UNIVERSAL LANGUAGE

Or
The Airlocked Room Mystery

UNIVERSAL LANGUAGE

LANGUAGE

Or
The Airlocked Room Mystery

Tim Major

NewCon Press
England

First published in the UK April 2021 by
NewCon Press
41 Wheatsheaf Road,
Alconbury Weston,
Cambs, PE28 4LF

NPN001 (limited edition hardback)
NPN002 (paperback)

10 9 8 7 6 5 4 3 2 1

ISBN:

978-1-912950-84-3 (hardback)
978-1-912950-85-0 (paperback)

Cover layout and design by Ian Whates

Typesetting and editorial meddling by Ian Whates
Text layout by Ian Whates

One

You know me.

I like to make myself understood right away. I like to make an entrance.

So there I am, banging away on a little door beside the cargo bay of the most decrepit Martian crawler base you've ever seen. Tharsis Caraway it's called, which is quite a sweet name for something so ugly. And not just ugly, but *big* and ugly. Maybe half a mile in length, though I'm not so good at estimating. Tall, too – I'm looking up and the place blocks out the sky. It's pockmarked with dents and the ventilators flap like trapped birds. Looks like it was once painted red but the storms must have put paid to that over the years, with only patches of colour in the odd crevice and the rest of it bare as a mole's arse. The sand's piled up against its huge caterpillar tracks – which are in bad shape too – up to maybe the height of a London bus, if that means anything to you. The dust has already begun to stain the glass of my helmet the colour of tobacco. It almost makes me want to sneeze even though my suit's pumping good clean air.

There's a comms unit beside the door, but I ignore it and keep bashing away with my fist. What's an armoured glove for if not for hitting things?

Still. I can't deny the wind's gone out of my sails by the time the little door starts to slide up. I step into the airlock, drum my fingers on the wall of the poky little space, sigh, wait for one door to close and the other to open, then step out of the other side.

Another couple of deflating sights: I'm standing in a featureless cargo bay and the welcoming party's just a lone guy. He must be some sort of engineer. He's wearing blue overalls and a collection of stains and a confused expression.

"Hello?" he says, peering up at me. It's not that he's short. My six-foot-three plus stomping boots tends to give me a vantage point.

"Are you the butler?" I say.

"What?"

"Would you be so good as to convey my calling card to his lordship?"

He just looks down at my gloved hand, held out empty.

"What?" he says again.

"Doesn't matter. What's your name?"

"Treadgold. Who are you?"

I shake his hand. "I'm Abbey Oma."

One of these days I'll say that and whoever I'm talking to will go, "Fuck, really? Abbey Oma? I've read all about you. I've seen all the shows they made about your exploits, on the box." One of these days.

But little Treadgold only says, "Okay."

"Right then," I say. "Take me to your leader."

"What are you doing here?"

"I'm taking off my suit."

And I am, turning my back on Treadgold but my guess is he can't help but watch. Not that I'm a pretty sight, mind you. I struggle out of the spacesuit and hang it on a peg which almost breaks under the weight. I hesitate, then transfer my pistol from my suit pouch to the one hanging from the belt buckle of my jeans. Even though my hair's short it's plastered to my forehead, and I haven't showered and my armpits are rank.

"There are no scheduled visits," Treadgold says. The poor love is stammering.

"That's right. This is an unscheduled visit."

"Where have you come from? Foxglove?"

I wave at the door. "Come on, Treadgold. You're sapping my will to live. Let's get going."

He stares at the airlock, then turns to gaze at the corridor that leads from the cargo bay. It's hard to know if it's me specifically scrambling his brains or if he just isn't used to talking to strangers, or people at all. Could be he's been relegated to cargo and never gets above the ground floor.

I take his hand and he looks up at me, blinking.

"Come on," I say in one of my nice voices. "Don't fret. What's your first name?"

"Franck. With a curly-cuh and a kicking-cuh."

"Cute. It's nice to meet you. Sorry for getting us off on the wrong foot. How about let's walk together."

We set off hand in hand and I swear I'm warming to him already. He's more like a puppy than a butler. He keeps looking up at me as if I might say 'well done' for putting one foot in front of the other.

When we get to the lift Franck's index finger wavers over the control panel.

"Top floor, I'm guessing," I say.

"You want management?"

"They'll want to see me. And as you say, there are no scheduled visits. So we need someone who can find a way to fit me into their schedule. I can see this place is frantically busy, am I right?"

The lift takes forever and it sways like a dinghy. Tharsis Caraway must be at least forty years old.

The doors open. Corridors, corridors. Where are all the people?

We end up in a big, fancy penthouse office. The floor-to-ceiling windows are scratched to buggery but there's decent views over the Martian landscape, and I guess I'm just that kind of person who appreciates barrenness. Out there it's all caramel-coloured rock and dust whirling around, carving more scratches into the glass even as I watch. Still, I'd take this over my view of three other prefab multi-residences from my flat in the Leeds suburbs. This room's filled with pot plants and sculptures. Obviously the plants aren't real. No idea about the sculptures; not my field.

At first it looks like there's nobody to greet us, but then I realise we're not alone. A woman wearing floral pyjamas is lying on a chaise-longue before the enormous window. There's a vintage magazine resting on her belly. Porn, is my guess.

"Would you do me the honour?" I say to Franck.

Poor Franck clearly wants to slink away back to the basement. I squeeze his hand.

He clears his throat. "Ma'am?"

Nothing.

"Ma'am?"

"What's her name?" I whisper, nodding at pyjama lady.

"Pannick. Edith Pannick."

I snort. "You're kidding me, right?"

Franck shakes his head.

So I shout, using two long syllables and taking five seconds or more: "Pannick!"

And of course pyjama lady does exactly that. She bursts up off the chaise-longue, eyes all wild, and instinctively shoves the mag down behind a cushion. She gives us both a cartoon-character double-take, then looks down at herself as if she's surprised that nobody thought to dress her while she was asleep.

"What on Earth?" she shouts.

"From," I reply. "And who."

Her eyes are still bulging. "What?"

I sigh. "Not 'what on earth?' A better question would be 'who from Earth?' It still doesn't make total sense, but at least I can answer it." I give her a chance to say something, but she was too busy blinking and gawping and smoothing down her crinkled PJs. "And the answer is Abbey Oma. From Earth, like I said."

"Earth?" she shouts.

"Shush. Look, you're scaring Franck." I give the little guy one of my best smiles. "Off you pop, Franck. It was lovely to meet you, but I think your boss and I can take it from here."

Franck can't believe his luck. Gratefulness seeps from his every pore. Without looking back at Pannick, he works his hand free of mine and scurries back the way we came.

"Nice boy," I say, and then I head over to the chaise-longue and sit on the cushion that's hiding the magazine. I figure it's better to leave the mag be and just enjoy the weird expression on Pannick's face.

"I'm here to see the body," I say. That's always a good way to kick things off, I've found.

Pannick gulps. "Which body?"

I raise an eyebrow. "The dead one. How many do you have?"

She shakes her head.

"You did hear about the corpse that was found in your base?"

"Of course," she said. Her cheeks are glowing. "I'm the senior manager of Tharsis Caraway. Nothing so important could escape my attention."

I shuffle my bum, turning to peer at the cushion I'm perched on. "I'm sure you're very attentive."

"But why are you here?" Pannick says hurriedly. "I don't mean to be disrespectful, but this man isn't the first person on Mars to die. Even in —" She stops, opening and closing her mouth without making a sound.

"Suspicious circumstances? Is that what you were going to say?"

"Unexplained. Unexplained circumstances is what they are. But even so, I mean, why are the Earth authorities sending someone now? It's been years since the last ship direct from Earth. And even that would have been trade rather than police." Her voice rises in pitch, ending up all squeaky.

"Pannick," I say, smiling. "Calm down. I never said I was police."

She's punctured, deflating before my eyes. "Oh. Right. Good. Well, in that case, I'd appreciate it if you'd state your actual business here."

"I told you. I've come about the body. Sure, I know there have been deaths aplenty in the colony. But even if the prospectors out there –" I point at the window. "– are dying in their dozens, they aren't your responsibility, and even though your employees here in Tharsis Caraway *are* your responsibility, I'll be straight with you: the authorities on Earth don't have enough hours in the day to care about randoms all the way out here in the backwoods of the solar system. Are you telling me you haven't reported the death, off-world?"

The mix of confusion and guilt on her face tells me the answer's no. Interesting.

"But if you're not police…" She looks me up and down. But all she finds is black vest, black jeans. No clues. Even so, she's sharper than she at first appeared. "You're an Optic, aren't you?"

I grin. "Rumbled."

"But working for who?"

"A little company called Sagacity?" I pull the paperwork from my pocket. It's crumpled but that doesn't reduce the impact one bit.

Those wide eyes again. "Shitting hell!"

"So can I take it that you'll provide me with all the assistance I may require?"

I bet she can't believe that only a couple of minutes ago she was asleep, dreaming her seedy dreams. "Of course. Anything you need."

"Right then. For the moment, best to keep schtum as far as off-world communication's concerned. Now, to the body!"

I stand and, I'll be honest, it's hard to resist the temptation to flip that cushion off the seat at the same time. But I'm not a cruel woman. I don't even turn to look at it. But the colour of Pannick's face brings me great joy.

Two

The trouble with these crawler bases is that they're basically ferries. They were designed to be on the move for a few months at a time – a year and a half, tops – and the facilities are obviously limited. But with Mars in the kind of trouble it's in, all those planned domed cities are stuck as blueprints for the foreseeable future. Sand-sculptor robots can build you a new structure every once in a while, but keeping them operational chews through cash, which is one of a bunch of things Martian settlers don't have. So most of these crawler bases ground to a halt, like old dogs flopping down before a fireplace, and more likely than not they'll never get going again. It wouldn't have been so bad if they'd coordinated themselves. They could have fulfilled the simplest part of the original plan, gathering together before they let the rust take over. No one would have been able to summon the cash to adapt the gathered crawlers into full-fledged cities as intended, but at least the residents of each base could have traded with each other, hung out for coffee, swapped apartments, spread the gene pools a bit. But as it is they're scattered around the surface of the planet, alone and sad.

My guess is that Tharsis Caraway's one of the saddest of the lot. Seems there's maybe a hundred people rattling around in a building the size of Bristol town centre. Nobody here's hopping out of bed each morning, clapping their hands in excitement about the day to come.

To make things worse, there are hints at what might have been. On my way down from Pannick's office I spot faded but once-colourful posters inviting me to explore the swimming pool leisure deck, the massage bay, the meditation suite. I pass a boarded-up set of doors with an unlit neon sign reading *Your*

11

Lucky Day and a smaller plaque below which says *No unaccompanied minors.*

But nobody around here looks like they're having a lucky day. My guess is that none of those facilities were ever built. They would have been developed once the crawler found a suitable location and, even more optimistic, its clientele.

In fact, I only encounter three people on my way to the morgue – a cleaner with a mop and no bucket, and two tweens trailing the caterpillar tracks of a sculptor robot like a skipping rope or a tripwire. Pannick's taken her promise of allowing me free rein so seriously that she shut herself in her office after I left and let me get on with it.

As I say, the facilities on these crawlers leave a lot to be desired, but even so I laugh out loud when I get to the morgue.

It's a kitchen.

I check the room code on the door – definitely the right place. To be fair, the work surfaces do look pretty clean. Somebody's keeping on top of that, at least.

I hear a sort of huffing sound and then somebody comes into the room, backwards.

"You all right?" I say.

"Jesus!" The man spins around.

It's Franck.

He's changed his clothes. Now he's wearing smart grey trousers, a nice white shirt rolled up at the sleeves. No jacket or tie. It only makes him look scruffier overall, though. His haircut's hardly a haircut at all. It looks as though it was shaved close a month ago, and then it all grew out in straight lines. I bet there's no hairdresser on board, bet he did it himself.

"No," I say. "I'm still Abbey Oma."

He pulls himself together. "Pannick sent word that I should help you in your inquiries. You know. Provide you with anything you need."

"I'm looking forward to working with you," I say, pretty much meaning it, because I'd definitely rather deal with him than Pannick. "So what's your actual role here, Franck?"

"Executive technical... something." His face flushes. "I can't remember what job title they gave me last."

I wave a hand, meaning *Why should I care?* but it could just as plausibly mean *Don't worry yourself over such a trifling detail.* I peer over his shoulder to look at the sack he's been dragging backwards into the room.

"And this is..."

Franck nods. "Jerem Ferrer. Give me a hand? He's heavier than you'd think."

Together we heft the body bag up onto the steel-topped kitchen island. An image flashes into my mind of us chopping up the body with the knives taken from the magnetic wall strip. Maybe Martian settlers will end up desperate enough for that sort of thing, one day.

"We don't use this kitchen for food prep," Franck says, seeing where my mind is going. "We have other ones. Lots of them."

My hand's on the zip. "Do you want to do the honours, or shall I?"

"You're the guest."

A body's a body, at the end of the day. I've seen plenty, and I suppose I've spent as much time looking closely at dead ones as live ones. There's nothing profound about that – it's just my job.

I already know that Jerem Ferrer's fifty-eight, but he looks a decade older, even if you discount the pastiness that eight days of being dead tends to bring out in anyone. He's wearing a thin white onesie and his cheeks are sucked in like he's expressing his disapproval about this whole affair.

I lift up one of his hands. The skin's papery and loose, though the flesh underneath seems bulgy, making the hand resemble a paw. The fingers are blue at the tips. Cyanosis, for sure.

"Anybody tampered with him?"

Franck's nose wrinkles. "Only to get him out of the suit."

"That was you? Why?"

"You can't bury someone in a space suit, oxygen tank and all."

I suppose that's true. Still annoying, though.

"No sign of a struggle," I say. No scratches, nothing under the fingernails. Just Ferrer's disapproving look, but that might easily be a side-effect of the asphyxiation. In Pinewood films, astronauts' eyes always pop out if they're exposed to the vacuum of space. But I'm not saying that's what I wanted to see.

Franck's standing to one side, watching politely. "Pannick said that you work for Sagacity."

"Sagacity's my current client. I wouldn't say I work for them."

"Still. Sagacity. That's a big deal. You must be good at what you do."

"Yeah."

"I hope you don't mind me asking –"

I give him a look. It means *Okay, sure, but any minute now I'm going to tell you to stop asking stupid questions.*

"Why are Sagacity so interested in the death by asphyxiation of a low-ranking – barely ranking at all, if I'm honest – scientific researcher on a crawler base in the middle of nowhere, on a planet with only one port, which hasn't seen any use in two years minimum?"

I nod, which isn't an answer to his question, only me agreeing that he's summed up the situation quite well.

"Because Sagacity, alongside being the world data banker, also retains a substantial interest in its historical core business," I say. "That is, the business that *made* it so rich in the first place, and the business that still drives its commercial operations."

It's beginning to dawn on him. He'll do as a sidekick.

"So you know what I'm going to say next," I say.

He nods. "You'd like to speak to the accused."

Three

Of course, we don't go to the cells, assuming there even are such things on Tharsis Caraway.

The workshop's littered with half-finished repair jobs: the raised skeleton of an AkTrak trundler stripped for parts, scratched-to-fuck window panes, countless black boxes with wires trailing. Oddly, there's a row of old-fashioned slot machines lined up against one wall. But more than anything there are robotic limbs: on work benches, on shelves, on the floor. Anyone working in publicity at Sagacity would have a heart attack.

Franck leads me past a row of lockers. Most of the doors are hanging open, and most of the lockers are empty. Even the ones that are occupied, I can barely make out the figures inside.

So you can imagine my shock on seeing one of them up close.

"This one," Franck says. He's stopped at a closed door with *Ai383* stencilled on it.

"Okay then. Open says-a-me."

The door swings open loosely, as if the hinges are about to go. The strip lights are all behind us, so the reason I can't see inside the locker is because of my own six-foot-three shadow.

"Stand back a little, would you?" Franck says. He taps a sequence into a keypad on the inside of the door.

There's a clanking noise. Franck flashes an apologetic look, reaches in, yanks something.

Then two rods come out of the gloom. Resting on them, with the rods under its armpits as if it's a gymnast on the parallel bars, is a robot.

And when I say robot, I don't mean anything you'd recognise as one these days. Nothing like you'd see on Earth, unless you were in a museum. Smooth fencing-mask face, pearlescent-white limbs: fine. But the weird thing is that it doesn't have hands.

15

Hands were too much for the designers to cope with back then. But you'd think they'd have given them *something*. Instead, Ai383's arms end at the wrists, making them look way too short for its spindly body.

"Aye-aye three-eight-three," Franck says. "Wake."

The first sign is that the ends of its arms glow blue, pulsing bright and dim, bright and dim. They suck a lot of the processing power, those blue circles at the wrist. In theory, aye-ayes can control any device in any crawler base, interfacing just by pointing a limb. In practice, the machinery in most bases became less and less technological over the years. If aye-ayes had emotions, they'd be livid that so many gadgets require fingers to operate.

The corners of Ai383's empty eyepits twitch.

"Are you there?" I say.

"I am here," the aye-aye replies. It's a too-smooth voice, a bit eerie. Nowadays, voice tech aims for functional, not friendly. For my money, friendly can be creepy, and I'm not sure I'm only talking about robots.

"I want to know what happened," I say.

Ai383 doesn't reply, but there's more movement around the part of its face where you can't help but imagine eyes. Maybe the lag's due to the ancient AI cranking up. Or maybe it just wants to consider its answer carefully before speaking. From the locker it must be able to see the spare-part limbs on the workbenches. If the threat of that fate isn't a death sentence, I don't know what is.

"This aye-aye was found –" Franck says.

I interrupt him. "I want three-eight-three to tell me."

The aye-aye says, "I was discovered in Jerem Ferrer's research facility, within an airless chamber, standing over his deceased body. I was holding his helmet."

"Two questions, straight off," I say. "Easiest one first. How can you possibly hold a helmet, or an ice cream, or anything?"

"Jerem Ferrer's helmet is of a generation of suits with which I may interface," Ai383 replies. "I am able to exert a magnetic force to lift it. When I was found, the helmet was suspended between my limbs, like so." Its arms bend, awkwardly because of the suspending rods, so that its blue stubs point at each other, a foot or so apart.

"All right. Question number two. Why did you start off by saying 'I was discovered'? I asked you what happened, not where you were found."

"I was discovered in Jerem Ferrer's research facility, within an airless chamber, standing over his deceased body." Exactly the same tone as before. "That is the truth."

I look at Franck and puff out my cheeks. "I'm going to stick my neck out here."

Ai383 raises its head to watch me closely. I should know better than to use idioms around robots.

"Blunt question, three-eight-three. Did you murder Jerem Ferrer?"

"It is impossible for me to cause harm to humans."

Franck says, "That's not an answer to her question."

I glare at Franck. If he's going to be my sidekick, he's going to have to learn some manners.

"That's not an answer to my question," I say to Ai383. "Did you murder Jerem Ferrer? No, hold on, I have a better question. Did your actions result in the death of Jerem Ferrer?"

Ai383's smooth face turns from me to Franck and back again.

Then it says, "I do not know."

"Why's that?"

"A hard reset has been performed. I have no memory of events before I was found in Jerem Ferrer's research facility, within an –"

"All right. Who's authorised to perform a factory reset?"

Ai383's head turns slightly. It's facing Franck now. So I look at Franck too, giving him the Columbo squint.

"The aye-aye only means that anybody can do it," Franck says hurriedly. "Isn't that right, three-eight-three?"

The aye-aye nods. "That is correct."

I squint some more. Always good to keep people on their toes. Then I say, "Could you have triggered the reset yourself, three-eight-three?"

"No."

"Are you capable of lying?"

"No."

"Perform diagnostic check."

After a few seconds the aye-aye says, "I am in optimum working order. All processes operational. No internal or external faults detected."

"Are you capable of falsifying a diagnostic check?"

"No. That would be a lie."

"And how do you feel about liars?"

Another pause. "I do not feel anything. But I cannot lie."

"Are you capable of running a simulation? If I tell you to shut off one of your internal processes, could you simulate it and then show us what would happen?"

"Disabling any core process would result in paralysis. If you were to do as you describe, I would be unable to respond."

I suppose I could have a go at disabling a few processes anyway, shut off a couple of baseline limitations, but that might well mean silencing the accused for good. Best not.

Franck is watching me with interest. "That tallies with all the documentation I've seen," I say. "And let me tell you it doesn't take long to read. These aye-ayes are rudimentary enough that core processes really mean *core*. Disabling any one of them would be like ripping out a human's spinal column."

"Thanks for that vivid image."

I turn back to the aye-aye. "We won't keep you much longer. How do you feel about being shut off while the investigation continues, by the way?"

Ai383's head lowers. Maybe it's looking at the suspending rods. "I do not feel anything. It is only appropriate that I am removed from service while the truth is determined."

"Okay. Last question: is your brain-pattern template intact?"

"Yes. Without an active template, my AI would be paralysed, other than a repeated verbal error warning."

Out of all the weird details about fast-tracking the aye-aye robots for deployment in the new Mars colonies, this is by far the freakiest. Each aye-aye's AI network is supported by, or resting on, or – I don't know, jumbled up with – a template donated by one of the original human colonists. It was the only way the techs could establish a basis for lateral thought, problem-solving, that sort of thing. Forty-five years ago, robots without that spark were just end-of-the-pier attractions capable of a single task. They were shit.

"And who was your brain-pattern template?"

"Felix Ransome."

"Hey Franck? Is Felix Ransome a resident of Tharsis Caraway?"

"No."

I look the aye-aye up and down. "You seem fine." I turn to Franck. "Doesn't he seem fine?"

"He?"

"Oh. Sorry. *She*, then."

Franck gives me a sizing-up look, then stares at the aye-aye for a bit, then shrugs. "So, what next?"

"First I'm going to ask you a long-shot question. Always start with a long shot. Are there are any records of three-eight-three's activity before the reset?"

"Nope. I've checked."

"Okay. Good. Never expect a long shot to give you anything. So we'd best be off then."

Franck hesitates. "To?"

"The crime scene, silly. Have you never *watched* a crime show?"

Franck tries to give a tight-lipped *do-try-and-act-like-a-professional* smile, but it comes off as goofy. You know me when it comes to awkward people like that. I feel like hugging him, but I *am* a professional so I rein it in.

"Come on then," I say.

Franck reaches for the locker control pad, but I pull his hand away gently. "Both of you. We're all going."

I wish you could've seen his expression. He's all flapping jaw and rolling eyes. "But it's accused of murder! It's not safe! Pannick would never allow –"

I shrug. "Always go with your gut. We both agreed that three-eight-three seems fine. And there's a distinct lack of other witnesses in this case, unless you happen to know of any?"

He shakes his head.

I lift Ai383 down from the suspending rods. She's a heavy girl.

"Go on, then," I say to her. "Lead the way, please. But as they say in the films: don't try any funny business."

Four

Corridors, corridors, and not a soul to see.

"So tell me about the aye-ayes," I say to Franck as we walk. "What do you use them for?"

"Well, back when the crawler was mobile — we came to a halt over four years ago — they'd be used for any external assessments and repairs. The storms were made far worse by us being on the move, because the caterpillar tracks would throw up dust constantly. Our suits could only withstand a handful of excursions before they'd get punctured. Aye-ayes might not be sophisticated, but they're hard-wearing. They also did a ton of work around the base, keeping everything ticking over."

"And now?"

Franck's eyes flick to Ai383 plodding ahead of us. "I dunno. They're just sort of *there*. Don't get me wrong, they're useful enough. Probably there's lots of things that would fall into disrepair if not for aye-ayes checking them over. I mean, our air supply, for instance. I don't know of any human crew member who ever takes it upon themselves to vet the recycling system."

"Huh."

Franck falls silent. You can just tell his mind's working away like a hamster on a wheel. "Huh," he echoes. "So if it turns out the aye-ayes are unreliable in any way — untrustworthy — then I guess we're in a heap of trouble."

I smile at him, because he looks like a kid about to cry. "Don't worry. We'll figure this out."

Plod plod plod.

"But hold on," Franck says. "That still doesn't explain why Sagacity cares about this. It doesn't explain why they went to the trouble of sending a freelance Optic all the way out here. Surely

Sagacity doesn't care about us, any more than anybody else on Earth cares about us."

"Fair point. Don't take any offence, though. They don't care about people on Earth all that much either."

A pause. "But Pannick told me you were asking about whether she's reported Ferrer's death off-world."

I don't reply.

"And she hasn't. Which is the answer you were hoping for, clearly."

"That *Sagacity* were hoping for," I correct him. I can feel my cheeks flushing. I don't like it one bit, being Sagacity's stooge, above and beyond the limits of my investigation.

"But Earth obviously knew about Ferrer's death – otherwise Sagacity wouldn't have known to send you. And if it wasn't Pannick who reported it, it was someone else, someone who maybe has an agenda."

There's no point arguing. Franck's sharper than you'd think. All of this is what you might call pertinent to the case.

We plod for half a minute in silence.

"Stop!" Franck says.

Ai383 stops immediately. Franck almost bumps into her.

He shakes his head. "No, sorry. I didn't mean stop walking. I meant 'hold on'."

Ai383 is as still as a statue, blocking the corridor.

"Carry on," Franck says. When the aye-aye sets off again, he says, "I meant I understand. At least I think so."

"Shoot, Watson," I say.

He scrunches up his face. It could be annoyance at my comment, or it could be him cranking up his hamster wheel of a brain. "Sagacity cares about whether aye-aye three-eight-three is capable of committing murder. And that's because they supplied the original AI architecture for the aye-ayes."

I wish I had a gold-star sticker to slap on his clean white shirt. "Okay."

"There's more? Of course, there's more. This isn't just about reputational damage. Even if three-eight-three could have done what she's accused of, Sagacity would have the means cover it up, buy people off, or even just deny it."

"I'm very proud of you. Keep going."

"But… but it's what this *represents*." Franck's going red from all the thinking. "If one of these earliest aye-aye models is capable of overriding its core limitations to murder a human, it's significant…"

I'm doing my supportive-primary-school-teacher expression.

"It's significant because… Surely not?" He looks up at me.

"Yeah."

His face goes all crumply. "It's significant because the newer models of robots, the ones on Earth, the ones that are all flashy and multipurpose… their AI routines are all modelled on the same architecture."

I'm rummaging in my pockets as I walk.

"What are you doing?" Franck says.

"Hang on." I pull out a £10 coin and hand it to him. "This is for you. You did good."

Ai383 turns left at a junction, then stops at a closed door and says, "We have arrived."

But Franck's just staring at me. "Seriously? The Sagacity techs never thought to clear the decks and start afresh? They just kept building new AI packages using the same old recipe – one that was cobbled together in a flustery panic maybe fifty years ago?"

I shrug. "Time is money, so they say. It's not a credo to which I subscribe. Money is money, I say. And time is the indefinite continued progress of existence and events that occur in apparently irreversible succession from the past through the present to the future. I got that from Wikipedia."

"Those fucking idiots," Franck says in a quiet voice.

"Yeah. Those fucking idiots, otherwise known as my current clients. Shall we go in?"

Five

It's clear at a glance that the research lab is sand-sculpted, and by that I mean it looks grubby as fuck. The walls are rough – still compacted and solid, but unpainted and lacking even a poster with a motivational quote to liven the place up. We're in a sort of lobby with a few desks and terminals, but the serious stuff obviously goes on behind the big curved window to our right. There's a ton of equipment in there. I dunno. Clamps and rods and beakers. Science stuff.

Franck sees me put my hand on the scratchy wall.

"Don't worry," he says. "Even though that corridor back there took us out of Tharsis Caraway proper, this place is all sealed against the elements. At least, this bit is. Here, we'd best put on suits now. Wouldn't want to open the wrong door while you're in your civvies."

I wish I hadn't left my own suit down in the cargo bay. You know me: I like my own stuff. Ai383 waits patiently while Franck pulls two grey suits from a peg on the wall, and hands one to me.

First off, it's too small. Once I get my feet into the booties, it gets so tight that it tugs on my shoulders, making me hunch up like Nosferatu. Secondly, it stinks. Whoever wore the suit last really likes meat. I take a deep breath before I pull on the helmet, and hold it in until the oxygen starts circulating. It hardly helps. I feel like I'm swimming in a gravy jug.

"Which suit was Ferrer wearing when he died?" I say. If it wasn't Ferrer who made this smell, I want to know who it was so I can keep well clear of them.

Franck clunks his helmet into place. "Neither of these. Had to cut him out of it. Couldn't get his arms out of the sleeves."

"But you checked it over?"

"Course."

"And I can trust you?"

He nods, but the helmet's so rigid that it doesn't move, and his forehead just taps against the clear dome.

There's something he's not telling me. Always best to clear the air, just like I wish I could inside this suit.

"Someone discovered three-eight-three standing over the body. Was it you, Franck?"

He glances at the aye-aye. "Yeah. It was me. But you don't have to —"

I hold up a hand. "I'm not. Don't fret about it. Some Optics like to assume everyone's guilty, then eliminate suspects. Not me. I prefer to assume everyone's my pal, but then reserve the right to change my mind if they... I don't know, blatantly lie, destroy evidence, attack me in my sleep. That sort of thing. Are you going to do any of that?"

His face has gone a funny colour. "No. I don't think I'll be doing any of that."

"Okay then. So, this is the way in?" I point at the only other door. Detective work just comes naturally to me. "After you, three-eight-three."

The aye-aye holds up its stub, which glows blue again as it interfaces with the controls. The door slides up.

Even though there's furniture and machines in here, it's also an airlock, a three-way type. That is, there are two more doors on the right and left. There are screens below each window, and even though they're turned off it's obvious they're intended to give more information than just 'door open' or 'door closed'. The little room we're in has curved walls and it's pointed at both ends, like an eye. Oddly, there's a comfy-looking red sofa at the far end, long enough that it doesn't really fit in the narrow space properly.

Through the windows to either side I can see into the labs themselves. The one to the right is the one I could see from outside, filled with the science things which are tethered to the floor with chains or else have huge, heavy-looking bases. The walls are even rougher than the ones in the lobby. In the middle of the domed ceiling there's a big hole – the room's exposed to the Mars atmosphere, and it's barely a room at all, just a sort of igloo-shaped enclosure. Hence the need for suits.

The left-hand chamber's different. It's the exact same size as the opposite one, almost entirely circular, so that the two chambers and the airlock together make a Venn diagram shape. But its sand walls are reinforced with smooth white plating – clearly, somebody didn't want to take any chances of air leaking out. Because there are lifeforms in there, a dozen or more.

"So these are the Martians I've heard so much about?" I say, pointing.

They're smaller than I imagined. In films, they're always shown as being the size of dogs, at the very least. But these crabs are... well, crab-sized. There's nothing much to write home about. They're redder than crabs I've seen on Earth (and when I say 'seen', I mean 'seen on my plate and then gobbled up'). They scuttle around half-arsed, bumping into each other even though the chamber's plenty big enough for the lot of them.

"In all their glory," Franck says.

"And there's air in there?"

Franck points at a readout below the window. Looks like healthy levels of oxygen.

"And how long has Ferrer been experimenting on them?"

"The whole time Caraway's been at its current location. Four years." Then: "Hang on. He hasn't been *experimenting* on them. He was just watching them."

I'm doing some watching, too. I'm watching Ai383, who's standing in front of the sofa as if she's considering taking a seat. She shows not a flicker of interest in what we're talking about, or even the crabs.

"They've all got scars, though, haven't they?" I say loudly, without looking through the window again. Still no reaction from Ai383.

Franck presses himself against the window so that his helmet tinks on the glass. "What? They look fine to me."

26

"Look closely. Just along the base of each shell."

There's a little line there, on each of them, on one side or the other, just above the point where the shell meets flesh.

"Huh. I've no idea what that might be about," Franck says.

"Lucky you've got an Optic on the case, then. Mystery is my middle name."

He gives me a look. He's still calibrating to my sarcasm.

"It's not really my middle name," I say. "My middle name's Francesca." It isn't that either, though.

"So, this watching. Is it something to do with this?" I'm kneeling on the sofa, looking down at a one-foot-wide transparent tube that runs behind it, leading straight from the air-filled crab room to the open-to-the-atmosphere chamber. Inside the tube are two shutters, slightly further apart than the length of one of the crabs. A little airlock for little Martians.

All in all, the lab looks a bit like this:

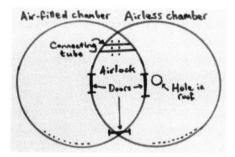

"There's nothing much to it," Franck says. "One crab goes into the tube at a time. Ferrer operates the airlock within the tube, to stop the air leaving the crab chamber. Then the test crab wanders on through into *that* chamber."

"Where there's no air."

"Exactly. Where there's no air."

"And then."

"And then he watches the crab."

"Which does what?"

"Nothing much. But it survives. That's the point. It's equally comfortable in the airless chamber as in the air-filled chamber. But nobody quite knows why."

"Because it doesn't need air, presumably."

"But that's just it. Look, I'm no scientist – I'm barely even an executive technical whatever-my-job-is – but even I get the gist of it. The Martians respire. They breathe, at least when they're over there where there's air. And when there's no air, they just *don't*. And wouldn't it be interesting to know why?"

I shrug. Knowing why things are isn't really my bag. "And just to be clear: you found Jerem Ferrer over in the airless room, with three-eight-three holding his helmet?"

Franck looks at Ai383 again. He's nervous now, as if repeating the accusation here might send the aye-aye schizo. "Yep."

Not a sausage from Ai383.

"Right then. Help me shift this sofa?"

Franck makes a meal of it, even though it's light. I could have moved it myself easily.

"Okay, let's see how this goes, shall we?" I say. "Three-eight-three, would you be a dear and get one of the Martians into the other chamber?"

Ai383 bows. Say what you like about aye-ayes, they have lovely manners. She starts interfacing with a panel above the transparent tube. One of the little airlock shutters in the tube lifts and there's another clunk, which must be the covering at the end of the tunnel. The crabs stop moving for a second, but then carry on bumping into each other.

"What now?" I say. "Do we have to coax one of them in? Stick a biscuit in the tube and say 'Hey, crabby, crabby, crabby'?"

Nobody answers, but it hardly matters. One of the crabs scuttles over to the tube entrance right away. As soon as it's inside, Ai383 seals the tube.

I bend close to look at the crab as it waddles through the narrow passage. Ugly little bastard, but fair's fair: he was here on

Mars first. The line on the base of its shell is hidden away on the far side. I tap the glass a few times, confusing it, until it turns around and I can see the line. Surgical, more or less straight, but made a bit bumpy by the scars as it's healed.

"You think it's a clue?" Franck says, peering at it too.

"Franck... *everything* is a clue." Then I laugh. "I'm just messing with you. It's the sort of thing Optics say. But all the same, yes. It's probably a clue."

The crab gets closer to the tiny airlock. When it reaches dead centre in the tube, Ai383 says, "Optic Oma?"

"You're so polite. Yes please."

She operates the airlock and the crab doesn't so much as flinch as the shutter slides closed behind it. There's a hum as the air is sucked out of the little space. You'd never know anything had changed, purely judging by the crab's behaviour. Once the door in front of it opens, the crab trots along the tube and into the airless chamber. Ferrer must have had the patience of a saint, watching that bunch of nothing every day for the last four years.

I stand up and check my suit. "Doors please."

Franck follows me into the airless chamber, but it's obvious he doesn't like being in the same room as the crab.

"Should I keep my distance?" I say.

"They're harmless," Franck replies, but he's still not taking any chances.

"Come on in and join us," I say to Ai383 just as she's about to close the door.

Franck's even more anxious now. "Look, Optic Oma –"

"Abbey."

"Abbey. Look, this isn't a good idea. I mean, these are *precisely* the circumstances in which I found Ferrer dead."

"Are you getting a nasty flashback? You should think about counselling. No good keeping things bottled up."

"No. That's not it. I just mean you're taking a risk."

"I realise that."

He doesn't seem to know how to respond.

I'm watching the crab out of the corner of my eye. It's pottering around the perimeter of the room, bumping into the metal stands every so often, but none the worse for wear. "Questions for both of you, then. Did Ferrer display any hint of suicidal behaviour?"

Franck shakes his head. "Not that I ever saw. He was absorbed in his work. In a good way."

"The same question to contestant number two."

Ai383 says, "I have no memories of Jerem Ferrer when he was alive."

"Second question. Can aye-ayes harm living things?"

"No," Franck says right away. "It's built into the basic template, even more fundamental than the human-donor pattern."

I look at Ai383.

"Yes," she says. "Aye-ayes are capable of harming living things, in particular circumstances."

"Such as?"

"In defence of a human. Or when acting upon a direct order."

I ignore Franck's shocked expression. "A direct order. And who could I order you to kill?"

"Not who, Optic. What. Upon a direct order I would be capable of harming, or killing, a lifeform that was sufficiently rudimentary as not to be listed on the charter of intelligence."

"What the hell's that?" Franck blurts out. It's an awkward moment, finding out that the robots he's been blithely knocking around with are capable of murder.

Ai383's tone is hilariously calm. "Officer Treadgold, there is no cause for concern. The charter of intelligence dictates which lifeforms have sufficiently developed mental processes to feel and understand their own pain. Upon a direct order, I would be capable of complying by harming a lifeform that was not developed to this degree."

I puff out my cheeks. "It's all getting a bit theoretical, isn't it? Shall we stage a practical instead?"

Franck looks lost, the little lamb. "What do you –"

"Three-eight-three," I say. I point at Franck. "Kill him, please. However you like."

Franck's eyes go all bulgy. He turns to stare at the aye-aye.

"I cannot," Ai383 says.

"There you go," I say, grinning at my Watson, who's suddenly got a very sweaty forehead. Then I rummage around in the pouch attached to my suit, where I stashed my pistol. When I pull it out, Franck makes a weird gulpy sound. He makes it again – a sort of backwards belch – when I point the pistol at the crab, which has conveniently come to a stop, tapping at the rough wall with one claw.

"Three-eight-three. I will shoot this Martian dead," I say slowly and clearly, "unless you kill Franck."

"No!" Franck yelps, and he jumps towards the door, hammering on it. "Three-eight-three, open this door!"

"No, don't open the door," I say to the aye-aye. I jiggle the gun. "I repeat, I will shoot this Martian dead unless you kill Franck."

It's as if Ai383 appreciates that drawing out the moment just makes it funnier.

"I cannot," she says finally.

I'm pretty sure Franck's going to be sick.

He jerks and almost falls on his arse as I pull the trigger. The shot's a bit off, hitting the Martian in its shell, but that's still enough to kill the crab. It makes a weird sighing noise and then its claws click onto the ground and stay still.

"What the fuck?" Franck shouts.

"See? So much easier to appreciate a practical demonstration. Hold on, nearly finished. Three-eight-three, please could you allow another Martian into this chamber? Thanks so much."

The aye-aye operates the tube airlock from a panel within the room. While we're waiting I keep the pistol more or less pointing at Franck, and I whistle a Moondog tune. Franck looks upset, maybe because I never was much of a whistler.

A second crab pops its head into the chamber and then hops down.

"Right then," I say. "Final experiment. Aye-aye three-eight-three. I will shoot this human dead unless you kill that crab."

"Good God," Franck says in a squeaky voice. "Optic Oma. Abbey. For the love of —"

"I repeat, I will shoot this human dead unless you kill that crab."

Ai383 doesn't move.

"Kill the crab, three-eight-three."

Franck watches on goggle-eyed as Ai383 finally approaches the crab. She bends, putting herself in its path so it starts to wander in a little circle within the curve of her white arms. Then she points both of her arm stubs directly at the Martian, either side of its snub head. Another sigh, and it's dead.

Ai383 stands. I'd swear something about her posture makes her look almost as rattled as Franck.

I put the pistol away. "How do you feel?"

"Fucking livid."

"Sorry, Franck. I was talking to her. How do you feel, three-eight-three?"

Her tone's as neutral as always. "I do not feel anything."

"Okay. I think we're done. Three-eight-three, please return to your locker and power down." I stand before the door, waiting to leave. "Franck, you should maybe get yourself a drink. And a shower."

Franck totters into the airlock, waits impatiently for the outer door to open, then rips off his suit and throws it on the floor of the lobby before dashing away along the corridor. Funny thing is, Ai383's barely any slower hurrying off. I think I've upset her.

Six

I find Franck in the bar. So *this* is where everyone is. The place is rammed, and dingy, and small. My guess is that the Caraway colonists like it this way, all huddled together in the dark. Makes it feel like the base is full of life.

They seem pretty much your typical stranded colonists. Lots of red faces – I bet there's a whole lot of homebrewing going on, on top of what they can get here at the bar. Lots of big groups, but plenty of people sitting on their own too. In a limited ecosystem, not finding your niche is a killer. I know because I've been there.

Franck's on his own, but not looking into his drink. As soon as I set foot in the place, he jumps up. I wonder whether he's been watching the door because he wants to see me, or because he doesn't.

"Before we start," I say when I'm close enough to be heard over the chatter, "there's something I'd like to say to you."

"Good," Franck says.

"Where am I supposed to sleep tonight?"

He blinks a few times, then sits down heavily on his stool. "And that's what you wanted to say?"

I take the stool opposite. A few people are looking at me. It's not every day someone like me wanders into a place like this.

"Settle down. Of course that's not what I wanted to say. My sense of humour gets me in trouble sometimes."

He's standing again. "Your sense of humour? Is that what you call it?"

By now pretty much everyone's looking at us. Part of the trick of being an Optic is making yourself the centre of attention, an authority figure. But you don't do it like this.

"I wanted to say sorry."

"For what, exactly?"

I point at the door. "All that business back there."

"Would you have shot me? Would you have let that aye-aye shoot me?"

"There was no risk."

He's shaking like a clockwork toy that's been over-wound. "It bloody well felt risky to me!"

I call the barman over and order a rum. He tells me it's not table service, but I know he'll bring the drink all the same.

"Franck," I say, giving him one of my best smiles, "I would never let you come to harm."

I can almost hear him deflating. He sits down and takes a gulp of his murky cocktail. "Too much bitters," he murmurs to himself. Then, to me, "You only met me a couple of hours ago." There's a hopeful upturn at the end of the statement.

"What can I say? I'm quick at figuring out who my friends are." It's true, and I do like him, his little blotchy face and his hair trying to escape from his head.

"Friends," Franck repeats, more in disbelief than any kind of agreement, but it's obvious that all is forgiven.

My rum arrives. I point at Franck, meaning *Put it on his tab*.

"So," I say. "Where will I be sleeping?"

Franck reaches into a pocket and pulls out a keycard. "The floor above this one. Don't worry, you won't hear the noise from down here, and there's nobody in the quarters either side. And it'll be clean, at least."

I pout. Is he saying something about my state of hygiene?

He gabbles, "I just mean that that's what we're all trained for. First and foremost, almost all of Caraway's personnel are trained in hospitality trades. That was supposed to be our destination, in career terms. A couple of years of crawling the sands, like a tour of duty – then, once a suitable location was determined, Caraway was supposed to rendezvous with at least three other crawlers, one of them a construction specialist. Once we'd docked it would have been a four-way marriage for life. We'd have built a city ready to host thousands of visitors at a time. We Caraway residents would've had a *purpose*. But it didn't work out like that. No location found, no funds, no docking, no friends, no tourists. We've no one to be hospitable towards."

I take the card. "I take it that some people left over the years?"

"Yeah. Whether they found anywhere better is a bit of an unknown. You do hear stories sometimes."

His voice sounds faraway, like someone reminiscing at the end of a life filled with regret.

"How old are you, Franck?"

"Twenty-three."

"And you were born on Tharsis Caraway?"

He sips. "It's that obvious? Have I got oversized eyes from being stuck here in the dark, or something?"

I don't say anything because I don't want to hurt his feelings. His eyes *are* weirdly big.

"I'd have been a barman, upon settlement," he says. "I had responsibilities while we were on the crawl, of course. Maintenance of the aye-ayes, mainly. But I'd only been working full-time for a year before Sandcastle stopped sending the base commands. We came to a halt for nine months and that looked like the end of it. Then Pannick got word of a new location scout investigation being set up somewhere over Iani Chaos way. She lobbied for the gig, and when he got it we had a hell of a party." He goes quiet, remembering. His cheeks flush. Maybe something else happened that night? My money's on him losing his virginity.

"What happened?"

He holds up both hands. "Caraway had already had fifteen years of service, non-stop with interchangeable crews, crawling the dunes endlessly. Turns out that the perfect location for a tourist hotspot doesn't exist on Mars, and what'd be the point, anyway, if Earth has no intention of sending anyone here? After nine months of inaction, Caraway was a ruin. Once we started moving again the aye-ayes did their best to repair it, and colonists were out on the hull too, hammering away, patching the holes, screwing loose nuts back on the moment they fell off. But you've seen the state of the exterior. Once the caterpillar-tread scales started dropping off one by one, there was nothing we could do. Pannick called in for replacement parts, the request got delayed, but by the time it looked as though she was making progress, Sandcastle had switched the orders to another crawler."

"Which is how you ended up here, in the middle of nowhere."

"Once we stopped, there was no one with the energy left to do anything about it. We were just waiting for some other crawler to find a location, hoping they'd call us over to join in, finally build a city. After a while the penny dropped. Since then we've just been waiting, but I don't think any of us really knows what for." He puffs his cheeks, then downs his drink. "Look, I've been thinking. About the case, I mean."

I've already finished my rum. I can't help looking at the door. But I force myself to say, "Go on."

He waggles his empty glass. I shake my head.

"That airless chamber," he says. "The aye-aye couldn't have taken off the helmet, right?"

I shrug.

"And Ferrer wouldn't have taken it off himself."

That's a stretch, but I let him carry on.

"So Ferrer must have died somewhere else, and then the aye-aye *took* him into the chamber."

I take a deep breath. There's nothing worse than explaining the obvious. "Three-eight-three is in perfect working order. If Ferrer was already dead, she would have been compelled to contact the base authorities. Who would that be?"

Franck swallows. "Me."

"But I trust you, and you weren't contacted, were you?"

"Yes, I was."

That deserves a raised eyebrow.

He shakes his hands from side to side like he's trying to scrub his words out. "I mean, I got an emergency bleep on my arm." He taps his bulky watch, which looks like one of those Casios you see in museums. The state of this place. "No specific code, just a location.

I was up in my office, so I went down to the lab and that's when I found the aye-aye standing over Ferrer's body."

"You have an office?"

He flushes. "Well, not *my* office exactly. It's shared, but I do leave my jacket there sometimes."

"Okay. Anyway, you've proved my point. As soon as three-eight-three woke from her reset, she saw Ferrer and called it in."

"Yeah." There's so much disappointment on that little face. "Okay. But I had another theory –"

"A theory?"

"Not a theory. A thought. What if it was an accident? What if Ferrer was in the air-filled chamber, the one with the crabs, and there was some problem with the airlock. Or with the tube that lets the crabs through! It could have let the air out, *whoosh*, and Ferrer didn't have his helmet on. And then when three-eight-three saw what had happened she dragged him into the other chamber, because she was, I don't know, confused, thinking the other chamber must be the one with the air in it. And then…" He trails off, but then his face lights up again. "The realisation about her mistake made her systems crash and reset."

I lean back, arms folded, nodding slowly.

"What do you think, Abbey?"

"I think it's a thought all right. But. After you left I checked the tube airlock, and the operating panel, and both were working as they should be. And aye-ayes don't panic and make mistakes like that, and the chambers don't actually look anything like each other, do they? And as we agreed, three-eight-three would have reported Ferrer's death immediately. Finally, if she was going to drag Ferrer out of the crab chamber and into somewhere with air, why wouldn't she just take him to the airlock and stop there?"

Poor Franck looks so dejected, I slip off my stool and give him a hug. Screw all those people watching.

"Right," I say into the hair on his head. "I'm off to bed."

Seven

But I don't go to bed. I've read Ferrer's emails on his lab terminal, so I know which are his quarters. There are more people milling around on the residential deck, so I do my usual routine: I whistle and look like I own the place. Of course, I still get looks – I'm at least six inches taller than any of them and, even though my hair's short these days, it being white tends to attract attention – but as I'm walking along I'm tapping the keycard onto my palm, peering at doors like someone wandering around an unfamiliar hotel, and that seems to keep everyone happy.

I wait for the corridor to clear before I break into Ferrer's room with my skeleton key. It takes all of five seconds.

Inside it's a mess. What would normally be a living room is basically an extension of Ferrer's lab. The wall's covered in whiteboards and pinboards, equations and spidery hand-drawn diagrams. I can't see a terminal. There's a mound of papers, and underneath it the suggestion of a desk.

I stand in front of the wall display, tapping my chin but basically only because I'm wondering what it would be like to be able to understand all those symbols and scribbles. Ferrer's drawn a decent cross-section of a Martian crab, just like the ones in school textbooks but with a big gaping hole under the shell, where the diamond would normally be. It's the pictures to the left of this that catch my eye, though. They're watercolours rather than pen drawings, and I'm no art-lover but they're kind of striking. You'd think maybe all those swirls represented the Martian dust, sent whirling by the motion of Tharsis Caraway, maybe. Except they're all the colours of the rainbow. Looking at the biggest picture, it's like I'm standing in the centre of a huge curling wave, ready to crash down and spill colour everywhere. Right there and then I decide that when this is all over, I'll steal it.

There's a clunk behind me.

"Who the hell are you?" a voice says.

I spin around. Standing in a doorway that leads into the other internal rooms is a young woman. Brown hair in a wonky bob, pale skin, wrinkled-up nose – although the last thing is probably only a consequence of her finding an enormous strange woman hanging around in her front room. She's tying the cord of a too-large blue dressing gown.

"Abbey Oma. Hi."

I'm impressed at how quickly she gathers herself. "And you're here because –"

"I'm an Optic."

"Ah. And of course Optics often go around breaking into people's apartments in the dead of night."

I tell you what, I can feel my cheeks going red. Something about that strict tone coming from someone in her twenties.

"I presume you're here to investigate Jerem's death," she says. It's not a question.

"I'm sorry for your loss," I say.

Her facade crumbles, just for a second. "Yeah. Thanks."

"You were his lover?"

She snorts. "What?"

"Wife, then. Or girlfriend. I don't know."

"No, you clearly don't. He was my uncle. He was almost sixty, for goodness' sake."

It's happening again. This makes two people I've liked immediately in a single day. There's something weird about this place.

I grin. "Sorry. I never was good at understanding people."

"And yet you're an Optic. I hope you have other skills to make up for the lack of that one."

I wonder if my smile comes across as creepy. "Even so, this is a small apartment for two people," I say.

She rolls her eyes. "I only moved in a couple of days ago. It's way bigger than my quarters. Uncle Jerem wouldn't have minded."

I nod. "Quite messy, though."

"I wouldn't change a thing. And I won't," she replies. She leaves the doorway to walk up and down before the wall display, her bare feet crumpling the loose sheets of paper on the carpet. She turns and holds out a hand. "I'm Hazel Ferrer. Please, do come in and make yourself at home."

I look around for a seat but there's only the swivel chair at the desk. I don't like the idea of sitting while she's on her feet.

"So, you're not from around here," Hazel says. "Let me guess. Earth?"

"Yup."

She's doing a bad job of hiding her enthusiasm. "What's it like?"

"It's incredible. It's like a theme park and a spa and heaven all rolled into one."

"You're making fun of me."

"Sorry. It's fine. It's just Earth."

"It's a hell of a lot more fine than Mars, is my guess."

"Mars has its charms."

"If you like sand, and big stretches of nothing, and being alone."

It doesn't sound so bad to me.

I clear my throat. "Do you know much about your uncle's work in the lab?"

Hazel swishes past me and perches on the swivel chair, then rearranges her dressing gown to cover her legs. I shuffle back to lean on the desk because hovering in the middle of the room suddenly feels weird.

"Sure," she says. "It's fascinating."

"Did he mention any breakthroughs recently?"

She shakes her head. "I'm not sure he even wanted to. If he'd come up with answers, he'd have had to stop what he was doing, or at the very least change the setup. He lived for his work. In fact, despite the mess in here, he rarely bothered returning to this level of the base. He'd have food delivered to the lab, and as often as not he'd sleep on a sofa there, just pulling a blanket over himself and then getting back to work after a few hours of sleep. He wasn't ambitious. He was just curious and he loved watching the Martians. They inspired him."

I glance up at the watercolours. "He was an artist."

"Not in the least. They're nice, though, aren't they? But everything Jerem put his mind to had scientific worth."

"So what are the pictures all about?"

I watch her as she gazes up at the wall. She has one of those faces you know won't change over an entire life, the same serious expression she would have had as a kid. She knows who she is, and she knows where she's going.

"We've all seen those images," she says quietly. "In dreams."

"What are they?"

"Storms. These pictures might not capture them perfectly, because they're static. In my dreams, they're always in motion. They're exceptional."

"And who's 'all'?"

She waves a hand. "Everyone. Everyone. A by-product of living on Mars, so we all assumed. Jerem had his theories, of course. He thought those dreams were put there, in our heads. By the Martians."

"Telepathy?"

"Yep."

"Why?"

She crosses her arms. "I trained as a linguist – I work as a speech and language therapist here on Caraway, one of only a handful of roles unrelated to the crawl or to hospitality – so my hunches would tend a certain way, regardless of my uncle's opinion. The first settlers spent decades trying to establish communication with the crabs, after they were discovered. Who's to say the Martians haven't been doing the exact same thing?"

"But do the dreams tell you anything?"

"Nothing we understand, no."

I consider that for a while, but Hazel interrupts my train of thought. "Is it true that everything's constructed organically on Earth now?"

I laugh. "Hardly. There are a few high-profile places — corporate headquarters trying to stand out from the crowd — that have been grown. But it's mainly a gimmick. Don't believe the pictures you see online."

"It's tough getting a stable connection these days. Even when I can access the off-world net, sometimes I'll find that the feed hasn't been updated for months. We're all but cut off, Abbey."

I hadn't asked her to call me by my first name, but I would have.

"Official status reports are still pushed to Earth by Sagacity," Hazel says. "Do they ever get picked up in the media? Does anyone on Earth…"

I can imagine the end of her question: *Does anyone on Earth still remember us?* And she wouldn't like the answer. I can't remember the last time I heard anything about Mars colonists, and the planet itself is only ever mentioned on TV shows as a historical quirk. As in, do you remember back when we all thought we'd be holidaying on Mars every summer? When we sent a bunch of people out there to colonise and construct, build the holiday chalets, turn down the bed linen? When the newsfeeds were full of footage of the crawlers scouring the Mars surface, hunting for ideal spots for a play park, a hotel, a leisure complex? The fact that the majority of those colonists never returned home is never mentioned, and the worst thing is that it's not from spite, it's because they've been forgotten.

"And how about everything else?" Hazel says quietly.

"There's been no wars for a good while," I say, offhand mainly because I hardly follow the news myself. "The European super-state is nicely established. People are hard up, though. Um. TV's not what it was."

It all came down to the economy, as always, making people conservative, more focused on themselves and their little bubbles. Money becoming tighter nixed any dreams of citizens holidaying on Mars, which in turn meant that the funds flowing to Mars dried up. There have been some good side effects of all the poverty, mind you. None of the sudden spate of international cooperation would have happened if countries weren't so bleak about the thought of spending big on another war. It was Mars that got the short straw.

"Okay." I can tell she's disappointed, but she's letting me off the hook anyway.

"And here? What's the gossip?"

"Apart from my uncle dying, you mean?"

"Sorry. Wasn't thinking."

"It's all right." She's teasing me. "There's nothing going on here. We're trapped, that's what we are. Cut off from our Earth family. The economy, such as it ever was, has tanked. Once we were definitively *not* going to become the solar system's favourite new holiday destination there was excited talk about the crawlers scouring the surface for signs of life instead. And then we *found* it, which only resulted in the most enormous who-gives-a-shit shrug from the home planet. We stopped generating interest, but we didn't give up. There's only so much you can do, though, isn't there? Once we'd swamped the market with Martian diamonds and their value dropped off, what did the planet have to contribute? Those of us stuck here aren't even worth the cost of the return journey. So here we all are, we brave pioneers, colonists of a dust planet that's going to remain dusty forever more. It's no wonder we're haunted by the storms, and it's no wonder so many of us turn to religion."

I raise an eyebrow. Nobody mentioned that in the briefing.

Hazel nods. "You should head on over to one of the revivals sometime. Every week without fail, and the congregation gets bigger each time. It's the only use our battered old fleet of AkTraks gets these days, ferrying folk over to Reverend

Guillaume's chapel. From what I hear, he's hardly unique. Even though we'll never get our big domed cities, the sand sculptors are keeping busy – but they're only building churches, cathedrals, temples, mosques. Nothing of any use, though I suppose that's just my opinion. Mars is littered with religious buildings and monuments nowadays. All funded by private donations, would you believe. People are desperate to have some place to call their own."

"And your uncle?"

Hazel shakes her head quickly, sending her already messy hair whirling. "Never. I guess that's where I get it. He's been my only family, my only role model if you want to put it like that. My parents died way back."

Well, anybody in the same position as me – orphaned, that is – gets a free pass.

I smile at her. "My parents lived here, too."

She's surprised. "Lived, as in past tense? They actually got home again?"

"No, but I did. Twenty-two, twenty-three years ago."

Hazel sucks on a strand of hair that's found its way into her mouth. "So this is like a homecoming for you."

"I suppose. I was only seven when I left. I don't remember a whole lot. I didn't have any dreams." I'm trying not to get sucked into all that nostalgia, because what's the point?

"But... Why did they send you back to Earth?" she says. "Alone, I mean."

I have my theories, obviously. I was never clear what Mum and Dad did for work. They sent me away well before Mars was clearly in decline; maybe they knew something that other colonists didn't? Not long after I left, the transit ships stopped and there'd have been no chance of returning to Earth for any reason.

That's what I *hope* happened.

"They never did tell me." I clear my throat, look at the ceiling. "Was Jerem happy, overall?"

"Of course. Nobody bothered him. He'd been indulged in his research by Sandcastle management for years, and there were no signs that he'd have to stop any time soon. Don't get me wrong, I'm not sure that's because anybody thought it was important or that it might produce useful results. It's just that he wasn't doing any harm, and his research didn't cost all that much once the lab was built. My guess is that Sandcastle liked the idea that there was *some* element of research still going on, despite the slashed budget. A middle finger stuck up in Earth's direction."

My stomach rumbles. Hazel stares at my belly and laughs. I think I might actually be blushing.

"The famed Caraway hospitality service isn't living up to its reputation, then?" she says.

"I forget to eat sometimes."

Hazel glances at the door which leads to the other internal rooms. The kitchen, the bedroom. "It's late. I've got plenty of stuff in. I'll rustle something up."

"You don't have to."

"I want to. You seem nice."

I can't remember the last time someone called me 'nice'. It feels... nice.

Eight

I'm stumbling my way along the corridor, bumping off one wall and then the other. The wine and the late night are part of it, but they don't go halfway to explaining my grogginess.

Those dreams.

It's hard to tell whether I would have had them anyway, or whether Hazel talking about them – and Jerem Ferrer's watercolours – put the idea in my head. But there they were all the same. They're hard to describe. A vortex, maybe, spinning around in front of me, but at times it felt as if I was actually looking down and the sand was like water rushing down a plughole. All the colours you can name, but the red was the most vivid. And it was *beautiful*. I woke up with a gasp and Hazel rubbed my back again and again. But I wasn't panicking, exactly. It just took a while for me to find my own body again.

Someone's walking quickly towards me along the corridor. They say a name three times before I realise it's mine.

"Abbey? I was looking all over for you!" Franck says. He's out of breath.

"Just woke up. Bit tired." I yawn and stretch to prove it, and my hands bash the flimsy ceiling.

"I was knocking on your door. When there was no answer, I got Services to bring a master key. You didn't sleep in your bed last night."

"I found a better one."

His sad little face. I could sleep with him, too, I suppose. He'd probably like that, and I don't much mind either way. But right now we have things to do.

"We're going to need an AkTrak with plenty of charge," I say.

"We?"

"You're my Watson, aren't you?"

"But I have a job to do here on Tharsis Caraway," he says petulantly.

I burst out laughing and after a few seconds he's laughing too.

"Okay," he says, relenting. "But where are we going?"

"To find some suspects."

He can't stop his face from lighting up. Everyone loves this sort of thing. I'm a very lucky girl, having this job.

"Who is it?"

"Who'd be top of your list to murder Jerem Ferrer?"

All that light suddenly disappears. He chews his lip. "He didn't have any enemies that we know of."

"Doesn't have to be personal. What did Ferrer represent?"

"His job, you mean?"

I nod.

"The crabs."

"Right. Who's most invested in Martians, other than Ferrer?"

Franck smacks his forehead. "Of course. Prospectors."

"There you go. How far is it to Xanthe Terra?"

I can see he's impressed at me having done my homework. "Three hours, four. I'll need to get Pannick's approval for requisitioning the trundler."

I pat him on the shoulder and it's all he can do to stop himself wagging his tongue like a happy Labrador.

"I'll meet you in the cargo bay," I say. "And as well as the vehicle, do me a favour? Bring coffee."

He gives a thumbs-up and then dashes away in the opposite direction.

I shout after him, "And a ton of biscuits!"

Nine

AkTraks are bumpy as hell, it turns out, and my hangovers hate bumps. No maglev, no suspension even. Each hillock under the caterpillar tracks produces a wrench and a vibration throughout the whole vehicle that echoes for a few seconds.

I wiggle to find a comfier position, what with all the shocks going through my bum. Franck notices. "You should have let the aye-aye drive. They're good at avoiding the potholes."

He's right, of course. The steering wheel's flimsy and unresponsive – it'd usually be folded away, only meant for emergencies. The driver's seat's rock hard because it's intended for robot arses.

"I figured you'd be happier without one of them as an escort," I say. "After yesterday."

"It's only three-eight-three I'm anxious about. You know, the murder suspect."

I don't respond.

"You don't think she did it, do you?" he says. "You don't even think we're looking for whoever gave commands to three-eight-three. You think somebody else was responsible, full stop."

"It's not my job to think," I reply. "It's my job to uncover the truth."

"That doesn't even make sense, Abbey."

I concentrate on the barely-there dust track ahead. Maybe I don't need a sidekick after all.

If I'm honest, those dreams are still getting to me. That dust storm is still whirling around in my head. There's barely a breeze out here beyond the trundler windscreen, but whenever I lose focus it's like I can see the red sand whipping around, and I catch my breath as if my throat might be clogged. Not a nice feeling, is what I'm saying.

I slow down for a team of three bulky sculptors that are busy smoothing the road where a storm has heaped up sand. If you think the aye-ayes are old-fashioned, these guys will take your breath away. It's as if somebody forgot to take them out of the boxes they came in – they're all right-angles. Their suction funnels are pressed into the sand like anteater snouts, and they're spraying the displaced regolith out of their rear ends.

"Do they ever actually sculpt, these days?" I say. "Or are they just glorified hoovers?"

"Not around here. They get hired out every so often, to private individuals. It makes Sandcastle a bit of cash on the side." He puffs his cheeks. "I say 'on the side'. Maybe it's Sandcastle's biggest revenue earner nowadays. Who knows."

We drive. I'm getting used to the AkTrak's controls. I swerve a bit to get the measure of it. Franck grips the dashboard with his right hand, leaning forwards at the same time to try and hide his instinctive reaction.

"Mind if I play some music?" I say.

"There's no stereo. The leisure vehicles were never built."

I grin. Optics have to be independent. I take one hand off the wheel and fiddle with my wrist panel, selecting tracks. I flip out the speakers from the base of the neck of my suit. Within a few seconds a Duke Ellington tune blares out, filling the cabin.

I swear it's the most impressed Franck's looked so far. We both nod in time to the music as we bump along.

You learn a few tricks. By far the most important is to provide your own soundtrack.

We drive. We eat dry biscuits worse than Rich Tea. Franck forgot to fill the flask with hot water, so all that's in there are dry coffee granules. We drive some more.

When the trundler's map screen shows we've entered the Margaritifer Sinus quadrangle, I turn down the music. "Tell me a bit about the prospectors, then."

Franck looks panicked. "I've never really met one."

"Breathe. I'm not accusing you of anything, Franck. And sure they're illegal, but not *illegal* illegal. Even I know they don't bother to hide. When was it that the first diamond was discovered?"

"Ninety-five. At least, that was the first time a member of the public discovered one. Who knows whether Sandcastle had wind of them before then? It'd been three years since the first crab was found, and there'd been rumours since then about what might be sitting in their bellies. My Dad was one of the folks who hunted Martians, in those early days. Did you know the first of them was found on Tharsis Caraway?"

I nod, even though I didn't know that.

"Little bit of history," Franck says, sounding far away. "So anyway, once the public knew that you could cut up a Martian and chances are you'd get a diamond, it became open season. It took a few years for entrepreneurial types to set up trawling trips, then a couple more for the base at Xanthe Terra to be established properly. By then the trawls were operated by the Prospectors Union, which sounds nice and official but of course when there's that kind of money at stake, it attracts crooked types. The Union were little more than a gang, a mob. There was no need for secrecy once they had the right people in their pockets, along with diamonds.

"And you were never tempted?"

"To go on a trawl? Dad did, again and again. It cost him everything he had. I never went myself."

Then Franck retreats into himself, and I don't have the heart to prod at him. Parents, huh?

Ten

It's only when Franck gets out of the AkTrak that I see the little yellow daisy painted on the right-hand side of his helmet.

"Did you do that?" I say, pointing.

His head turns within his helmet, but of course he can't see the outside. His cheeks go red all the same. "A tiny act of rebellion, years back. It won't come off, which is kind of hilarious given how the dust has scoured every trace of printed text from my oxygen tank."

"I like it," I say. "I'm glad it didn't come off."

I take his hand. Then, as if we're doing a choreographed dance, we each use our free hands to shield our eyes against the red glare coming from the east. Pearl Bay is bigger than I'd expected, but even from up here on the hillside it's obvious which part was built to a plan and which is the shantytown that grew up around it. In the centre, the camp's built on a thick base plate – sand-sculpted rather than metal, presumably, but it still must have cost a fortune. All the huddled tents and shacks beyond it are teetering on any surface to hand – bits of old sand walls, metal plates stolen from crawler bases – and some are self-contained structures resting on nothing but the sand. It's hard to imagine sleeping in one of those tents during a storm. The way the sand barchans shift around, you could go to sleep on the outskirts of Pearl Bay and wake up in Arabia Terra.

It's in a state, though. Curved struts like the ribs of a huge whale arch over the base plate, but there's no roof between them – even if the base plate still rotates, there'd be no protection against the wind. Back when the diamond industry was thriving, this whole place would have been buzzing, and I guess all those structures would have needed constant maintenance. Some of the sand-sculpted buildings on the base plate seem in decent nick, but

51

the ones on the edges have been left at the mercy of the dust. There are roofs missing, walls with holes punched through.

"Don't judge," I say. "Maybe the neighbours are nice."

We trudge through the sand, shaking our feet above the surface after each step to stop us from sinking. Franck's a foot shorter than I am, and I have to pull him free a few times. When we arrive I lift him up onto the base plate and pat him down.

"Where to?" Franck says, turning around. My guess is he doesn't want me to see his face, what with me treating him like a kid.

"A place like this? Follow the smell of alcohol."

Franck taps the glass of his helmet. "But I can't –"

"Figuratively."

"Oh." He's none the wiser. Then he sees what I see. In the direct centre of the camp is the only building that matters, a big sand igloo. There are red lights in the tiny porthole windows. "Figuratively."

He lets me go in first, a total gent. Even without my suit on, I'd have had to duck to get through the door. Once we're inside the place feels bigger than you'd expect. It's a single large room, dark, lit by fizzing red lights like the ones miners use. To our left is a long bar counter, designed to serve maybe ten people at a time. The bottles are still racked up on the wall behind it, but even at a glance it's clear they're empty. In the middle of the room is an untidy pile of stuff. It doesn't look valuable. More salvage, maybe parts of the original camp canopy, bundles of clothes, crates that might contain bottles or maybe weapons. Nothing unusual.

"That reminds me," I say quietly. "Did you think to bring a gun?"

Franck's wide-eyed. "You think I'll need one?"

I shrug. "Doesn't matter. Don't worry about it."

His mouth opens and closes. That's him put on the alert for any trouble, then.

Beyond the heap of goods is a cosy area filled with sofas – or rather, rows of seats ripped out of public-access trundlers, but it amounts to the same thing. They look a hell of a lot comfier than what I've been sitting on for the last four hours. Even so, the little area doesn't look all that welcoming. Sitting on the seats are a man and a woman whose faces are more scars than clear skin. They stand up slowly as we head over.

"You travelling?" the man says. He's not far off my height, shaven-headed inside his battered helmet. He's scrawled symbols all over his suit – they look a bit pagan, but not in the nice hippy way.

"We have been," I say. "And this chap didn't pack drinks. Any chance of a little something?"

The woman nods. Her eyes keep rolling back in their sockets. "Sure. If you're a customer."

She doesn't mean a bar customer. She means the other kind.

"Water will do," I say. "But don't worry, we can serve ourselves. Franck, head on over and get us both some water, would you?"

Franck stares at me, then at Mr and Mrs Scarface. Before he slips away to the bar, I pull out the flask from my pouch and hand it to him. "Make it hot water and fill this up? I really do need some coffee. We don't want me getting any more cranky than I already am."

The prospectors are such a mess it's hard to read them. They might be impressed or they might be riled up.

"I'll ask you again," the man says to me, "Do you need transport?"

"There's nothing to be caught here at Pearl Bay?"

He shrugs. "You got a net?"

"Nothing bigger than a sieve. Actually, I don't have a sieve either. I don't know why I said that."

"Then you'll need to travel to camps that still trawl. We can point you towards three that'll be active today, and provide transport. You won't find them any other way."

"You have a ship?"

The woman cuts in. "Trundler fleet's the only way to travel. It's all about weight distribution." She struggles with the last word, but it's clear that if she wasn't dosed up, she'd be smart enough.

Franck comes back with the flask. I wink at him, then hold up a hand to pause the conversation as I fumble to hook up the liquid tube on my suit, then divert the liquid intake. I slurp coffee through my helmet straw and then do a goldfish impression. "That's *hot*!"

"Do *you* have a ship?" the male prospector says.

He's done nothing to hide the tapping on his wrist computer while he was talking. I raise an eyebrow to show I've clocked it. "What makes you say that?"

He reaches out to tap me on my chest. That's taking liberties, isn't it? "The Europus flag. That suit's new. You're from Earth."

"Busted."

The woman comes close to peer at the tiny flag too. "Fuck. They finally sent someone?"

"Yeah. Some *one*. I'm an Optic. Abbey Oma. It's a pleasure to meet you."

Both of them grin suddenly. The man gestures with his bulky gloved hand. "This is Clem and I'm Munch."

"As in the painter? The Scream?"

He shakes his head, then parts his lips to show me his rotten teeth. "As in *munch munch*."

"Well, like I say. An absolute pleasure. Isn't it, Franck? This is Franck, by the way. He's not an Optic. He's my friend."

Franck gulps, holds out his hand to shake theirs. When neither of them take him up, he freezes like that for a moment, then wraps his arms around himself.

Out of the corner of my eye I see another two suited people duck into the room. They're standing either side of the exit like bouncers. They're big fellas.

"So, then," Clem says.

"Yep," I say, nodding. "So."

There might well be more thugs waiting outside. There's probably nothing but thugs in this whole camp. Nice word to say, *thugs*. I take a seat and gesture for Franck to take one too. After a few seconds of glaring, Clem and Munch perch on the seats opposite, but their feet are planted on the floor, ready for action.

"Franck here's been telling me about the diamond industry," I say.

"You thinking of investing?" Munch sneers, showing his teeth again, red light reflecting from metal fillings.

I ignore the question. "He tells me there's not much money to be made these days."

"Unless you're buying," Munch replies.

"Oh, I'm wealthy all right. But I left my purse at home."

Clem leans forwards. "At home, or on your ship?"

Munch glares at the back of Clem's helmet, obviously annoyed at her being so blunt.

"Before we get to that," I say, palms held out, "I have a question. Do you know Jerem Ferrer of Tharsis Caraway?"

They look at each other. Munch shrugs. "Yeah."

"Do you like him? Oh, he's dead, by the way."

I watch their faces carefully. There's nothing going on with Clem's, but that could just be the drugs. A flicker of a reaction from Munch, but I'd swear it wasn't guilt.

"That's why you're here?" he says.

"That's why I'm here. Suspicious circumstances."

Munch's facade drops. "Ah, fuck."

I don't say anything. There's a time for just looking.

Franck obviously feels he should contribute to the conversation. "What was your relationship with him?" he says, then looks at me for approval. I shrug. Everyone has their own technique.

Clem looks back at Munch, who's slumped in his seat. "Business," she says. "It's no big secret. We make a fair bit out of Ferrer. I mean made."

I nod. "So you're the ones who've been supplying him with Martians?"

"Yeah," they both reply at the same time.

"And you're the ones who made the incisions under each of the crabs' shells?"

Munch nods. "We weren't even cheating him. The first batches we gave him, the diamonds were still in there. But he ordered more and more, and I just went and asked him outright: 'How about we extract the diamonds first?' And he didn't give a shit either way, as long as they were supplied alive. If ever there was a win-win situation..."

"I did it myself," Clem says, holding up her hands. Presumably when she was wielding the knife, she'd have made sure her hands were shaking less than they are right now.

I slurp coffee, then put the flask away and slap both hands on my knees. "Well, there we go, then. That's that cleared up."

"You're not going to take us in for questioning?" Munch says. That sneer again.

"I'm not a cop. But no. All above board here. Other than the illegal crab-hunting and bribery and gun-running, I mean."

I get up and tug Franck to stand too. Neither Clem or Munch move from their seats. I sense the bouncers behind me leaving their positions at the door, coming closer.

"See, here's what's about to happen, Franck. Just so you're prepared," I say, without turning to look at him. "Our new friends are going to attack us, and they'll capture me – and maybe kill you, because you've not got much to offer, let's be honest – and then they'll force me to let them board my ship to leave Mars." Then, to Clem and Munch, "Am I close?"

"Yeah," Clem says. "Very close."

I put my hand on Franck's arm. I can feel his trembling through the suit. "It's all right. It won't work."

"Why's that?" he says in a tiny voice.

"Because the forces of good always prevail? I dunno. I'll think of something."

The bouncers are almost on us. Clem and Munch jump to their feet and at the same moment I reach for my pouch, and then I can't help but grin at the thought that I might accidentally pull out the flask of coffee instead of my gun, and then all my confidence disappears in an instant as something grips my arm before I can level the pistol. Ah, fuck. I turn awkwardly to stare into the eyes of some guy I hadn't noticed before. Bloody helmet blocking my peripheral vision. His face is red from holding my arm still, but in another couple of seconds the back-up arrives. One of the bouncers pins Franck's arms effortlessly and the other takes my gun and looms behind me.

"Like Clem said, you're very close," Munch says, scuttling over to stand right in front of me – two more inches and our helmets would bonk together. "But the twist is that we don't actually need either of you alive."

It's a fair point. "Because as long as you have my suit ID, you can chop off my head, or pull out an eye, and that'll do for the retinal scan."

"That's about the size of it."

"Huh."

Franck manages to turn within the bouncer's embrace. "Abbey?"

"Don't worry, pet." But that won't stop him worrying. People like Franck aren't capable of seeing a way out of a situation like this. So I add, "I'll count to three, and then we'll leave. Okay?"

"Okay." He draws the word out, making it last.

"One."

Munch and Clem exchange looks. Mainly disbelief, but my hunch is they've taken a shine to me. That doesn't mean they aren't going to murder me, mind you.

"Two."

The bouncer and the out-of-the-shadows thug are each holding one of my arms now.

I don't say three. Always give yourself the element of surprise.

First off, I let the meatheads take the weight. My body sags, my legs buckling under me. There are twin *umph*s from either side of me as the thugs strain to keep me upright: you know me, I'm a big girl. I give them a second to pull themselves together – now they're holding me suspended like a washing-line between them – and then I do a tidy bunny-hop off the ground, kicking out with both feet as I rise. I aim for their crotches, for what it's worth, even though their suits are sure to provide padding – but like people say, reach for the stars. The sound they make is more *what-the-effing-hell* as opposed to *ow-my-fucking-cock*, but that'll do for me. They're not down but they both stagger back.

This time I'm counting in my head. One, two. Still no three. Sometimes it's best to surprise yourself too.

I throw out both my arms suddenly. Double *clinks*, then gasps. I indulge myself by taking a look at each of the thugs. My armoured gloves aren't tough enough to punch directly through the glass of their helmets, but as I watch the spiderweb cracks get bigger and bigger. Both of the bouncers are clawing at the glass, as if what's happening is a nosebleed and a pinch of the nose might stop it. They look at each other, eyes wild like they're high – and maybe there's enough of an oxygen leak that they *are* high, suddenly – and then they stumble away towards a back room, bumping into each other as they go.

All that happened in maybe five seconds.

Munch is clinging onto Clem's arm. He's too sober to even think of taking me on, and she's too wasted. But they both keep looking at the back of the sofa. There are guns back there, I'll be bound.

The third and final bouncer pulls Franck into a clumsy human-shield position. Franck's barely had time to process what's going on and he lets himself be pushed around. His limbs have gone all saggy. I can use that.

"Protect your head, Franck," I say.

He puts his hands over his eyes, as much as the helmet lets him. For a second I just watch him, my heart swelling like an indulgent mum's. You've got to love Franck.

The bouncer's expecting an attack from the front, of course. So in one quick movement I dart around to one side and he wrenches himself around to follow me, but I'm behind him before he's cottoned on. I only have a few seconds before he braces himself, and if I hit him he might easily crush Franck.

So, instead, I scoot down and reach through the bouncer's straddled legs. Franck makes a high-pitched squeal as I pull his ankles towards me, and then he's falling forwards, fast. I'm guessing he kept his hands up like I told him to, because the sound he makes on impact with the hard floor isn't a full-on crack, but he'll have bruises. I yank his ankles, sliding him through the bouncer's legs, and then in one nifty movement I swing Franck up onto his feet again. I put myself between him and the three prospectors. By now Clem and Munch have drawn their guns. The bouncer looks to them for instructions but their eyes don't leave me.

There's only one thing for it now. I hold up both hands, still blocking their view of my Watson.

I push Franck behind the pile of crates at the same time as I leap towards the nearest one myself. Bullets pop into the crate lid the second I lift it up.

I had a fifty-fifty chance, but instead of weapons, the crate's full of bottles. If Caraway had ever settled to become a hospitality hub, my guess is that the prospectors would have hoped for a place in the supply chain.

I'm a bit disappointed, but still. If life gives you lemons, make lemonade, and if life gives you flammable liquid, make a big fuck-off fire.

But I need a light.

The bullets are thwacking into the metal lid as I fiddle with my wrist device. I rip off the fascia and prod at its internals with a finger that's maddeningly fat because of the glove. I hit the device against the sharp corner of the crate, and something sparks.

"Back up to the exit," I say to Franck without looking at him. "And keep me between you and them."

I stand up. Munch's nose wrinkles when he sees I'm holding a bottle in each hand, and both him and Clem stop firing for a moment in their confusion. Booze is flowing out of each upturned bottle. This bootleg homebrew had better be potent, or I'm screwed.

I drop, grabbing two more bottles and then touching my sparking wrist device to the puddle I've already made.

And then there's a lovely *whoomph*.

I don't even check to see their reactions. They're out of practice at all this sort of thing, is my guess. When the food chain disappeared they became foragers rather than hunters. As I sprint to the door a few shots come my way, but they're halfhearted and only one hits me, in the thigh. I hold my breath, ready for the air to get sucked out of my suit.

Franck's a mess, spinning on the spot outside the union building. Gently, I turn him so he's pointing the right way, then give him a friendly tap to get him going.

As we jog off the base plate and clumsily up the dune to the AkTrak, a bell's tolling somewhere and I see a few people leave their shacks, heading to another intact sand-sculpted building with a wonky steeple. They look straight ahead and either don't notice us or don't want to.

Eleven

Franck drives while I root around in what you might as well call the glove compartment. Finally I find what I need: a big roll of silver tape. It takes me a while to find the free end of the tape with my fat fingers, and it's all I can do not to swear. Finally I manage to pull off a piece and stick it over the hole in the leg of my suit. Even though my wrist device is broken, within seconds I can tell the oxygen level's returned to more or less normal. I take a deep gulp of air.

Franck looks sideways at me. "Are you okay?"

"Fine, thanks."

"But you got shot."

I wave a hand. People get shot all the time.

"Did it... go through you?"

"There's only one hole in the suit, so no."

"That means the bullet's still in your body."

"It's not the first." I'm not just showing off. I really do have two other bullets still inside me somewhere. I forget where.

"We need to get you to a medic."

I blow through pursed lips. "Maybe later, when we get a free minute."

Franck turns to look out of the back of the AkTrak. "Nobody's coming after us."

"The prospectors knew it was a long shot. They'd have figured it was worth a try to get off-world, but they won't bother us again."

"But you think they would have gone through with it? Killed you to get your ship?"

"They're as sick of Mars as anyone. And they're more childish. Yes, I'd say they'd have done it."

He stares at me. "*Childish?* Abbey, they wanted to cut off your head."

"Yeah. Silly billies. By the way, we should be going west."

Franck pulls the wheel sharply to the left, almost overturning the trundler. He's probably never driven one before.

"Your hands should be at ten to two on the wheel," I say quietly.

He renews his grip on the wheel and instantly the ride's smoother. We travel in silence for a while, but then he thumps the dashboard and whoops. "I can't believe we got out of that mess!" His voice lowers again. "How are you going to get more information out of the prospectors, though, for your investigation?"

"No need. They're eliminated. They're as honest as the day is long."

"Because they were making money out of Jerem Ferrer?"

"That, and because they're not smart enough to use him for anything bigger. You saw Munch's delight that Ferrer hadn't argued about them taking the diamonds before handing over the crabs. I think he really liked Ferrer, or at least liked the sense of conducting an honest deal and *still* winning, even though silicon diamonds are worth peanuts nowadays. The prospectors are in a tight spot now that Earth won't pay big. They're so desperate they'd take any opportunity that arises, including going straight." I point out of the windscreen. "Leave the track and head towards the sun. Maybe pull the visor down, drive safe."

Franck does as I say.

As we leave the sculpted track we pass a sand-bleached billboard with a barely-legible sign advertising the Daisychains spa resort, the name flanked by faded palm trees. I went there when I was a kid, not long after it opened. A vision of the future, they called it. It was impressive, especially the amount of greenery imported from Earth and crammed into the central leisure dome with its jacuzzis and waterslides. But even as a six-year-old I could sense it wasn't sustainable. It wasn't just the amount of water being pumped through the system every hour to keep it all running. Even back then I could see the place straining at the seams, the disarray hardly even hidden behind the fancy facade. The Daisychains resort had been pulled together in a desperate hurry, a last-ditch attempt to demonstrate to Sandcastle and Earth that Mars was a viable holiday destination. We had a fun day, though, me and Mum and Dad.

Franck interrupts my daydreaming. "Where are we going?"

"Sandcastle HQ. By the way, who runs the show these days?"

"Felix Ransome."

"What? The same guy who donated his brain patterns to aye-aye three-eight-three?"

"Yep, but don't read too much into that. Ransome was eight when he arrived with the first batch of colonists. An evacuee, an orphan. All of the first colonists' brains were scanned, and Ransome, being young, was a prime specimen. His brain patterns underpin loads of the original aye-ayes that were on that pioneer expedition."

It's a funny coincidence, Felix Ransome being shipped off-world without his parents. The same as me, but going in the other direction.

In fact, Ransome's name has been ringing a bell since Ai383 first mentioned it at the base. Now I remember. In the lobby of Sagacity's corporate offices on Broad Street in Oxford there's a statue, sand-sculpted by prototype robots maybe sixty years ago. It shows two figures: a man standing with his back to people entering the building, his head tilted as he gazes up at an oversized humanoid which is half-finished, limbless, the machinery within its skull exposed. Beneath it is a plaque that reads *Elias Ransome, Father of Modern Robotics*.

And father of Felix, too, as it turns out.

Twelve

Sandcastle HQ is nothing like Sagacity's vast glass offices. I'd expected that – but I'd figured it would be either a sand-sculpted building or a handful of crawler bases bolted together, the usual method of cobbling together makeshift Martian cities.

I check the coordinates on the dashboard screen as Franck guides the trundler along the driveway, which is so smooth that compared to the bumps and jolts so far on the journey it feels like we're skimming an inch above the ground. On either side of us are rows of trees.

"Hey. Stop for a sec?" I say.

I hop out, wincing a bit at the pain in my leg. I change my hobble into an only-slightly-awkward stroll in case Franck's watching.

The trees are all different species. I head over to the nearest one, a birch. Its bark is flaking away like paper.

I tap the shining white trunk. It makes a dull sound. Then I tug at one of the flakes of bark. Solid. I pull harder and it comes away, but with a brittle snap rather than tearing. When I rub it between my gloved fingers, it crumbles.

I stretch up to the branches, and grab at a mottled yellow and green leaf. It clips off neatly, shearing from its narrow stem. I turn and head back to the trundler, holding the leaf between my thumb and index finger for Franck to see.

He leans over from the driver's side to take it. He frowns and gives it an exploratory wiggle. His look of dismay when the leaf snaps in two is so adorable that I decide right there and then that he's my new best friend. He stares forlornly at the dust in his lap.

"It's made of sand," he says. "But why?"

I look around at the other trees dotting the driveway at five-metre intervals. Alder, willow, hawthorn, crab apple and more.

Some of their branches are bare and the feet of a few trunks are surrounded by leaves, simulating the first days of autumn.

"Test cases for tourist attractions, maybe," I reply, "or just plain old nostalgia."

I get back into the trundler. After a minute we're clear of the trees and we can see our destination.

I assume it *is* sculpted from sand, though at a glance you'd never guess.

I've seen places like this, but only on TV. The real things probably still exist on Earth, in remote areas where rural billionaires own the surrounding land and can hold off the expansion of nearby suburbs.

I suppose it's what you'd call a country manor. As well as a wide, three-storey central part, there are two lower wings that spread out either side, angled around a paved turning circle filled with colourful plants and a statue of a kid. The thing that strikes me is the number of windows. There are maybe twenty-five of them visible from where we are, all narrow and crosshatched with fake lead. Presumably behind each one is a *proper* window, reinforced to withstand atmospheric pressure, but the facade's convincing. The stonework must be painted sand, like the trees. What looks like limestone is mottled and discoloured, chipped at the corners. This decay hasn't been caused by Martian dust storms, because that would have exposed the real caramel colour of the sand rather than this speckled grey. I can't imagine how many aye-ayes it'd take to repaint the manor after each storm, which come around maybe once a fortnight.

Franck is so intent on staring up at the house that he almost drives straight onto the roundabout filled with flowers. I lean over and kill the engine.

"I guess Sandcastle isn't just a fun name," he says quietly.

I laugh. He's all right, Franck is.

I get out but Franck hesitates. "I still don't have a weapon."

I walk around the trundler, open the door and help him out. "You can't go around with that kind of attitude. You have to learn to trust people."

"But what about those prospectors back there? It wouldn't have been a good idea to trust them, would it?"

"Fair enough," I reply. "You have to know *when* to trust people. But here's the thing. If you go around waving guns in people's faces, you won't be able to blame them if they try and kill you right back."

With that, I head towards the manor. Fifty quid says Franck's frowning at my pouch that holds my pistol. I never said I wasn't a hypocrite.

The entrance sticks out of the middle of the house front like a permanent drawbridge. Its roof is supported by Greek columns. Probably all this is mainly to hide the main doors from view when you approach the house, because when we reach them it turns out they're disappointingly functional. I can't see a camera but I figure there's one somewhere.

"Optic Abbey Oma," I say. At times like these I wish I had a badge to hold up, but what's the point when there are retinal scans and facial recognition AI?

Nothing happens. I turn at the sound of footsteps behind me. "Oh, and Franck."

The airlock doors slide open. In we go.

Once we come out the other side of the white box, the whole country manor thing is re-established. The floor of the lobby is tiled, and in its centre there's a large, intricate mosaic of a fox sitting on its haunches. It's dim in here – as I thought, the windows we saw from outside don't actually let in sunlight. The only light is provided by lamps with stained-glass shades, which make the lobby feel like the inside of a kaleidoscope. The walls are covered with paintings, mostly British landscapes.

Franck almost jumps into my arms when an aye-aye pads out from one of the adjoining rooms.

"Hi there," I say. "We'd like to request an audience with Felix Ransome,"

The aye-aye bows and turns to the central staircase at the far end of the lobby.

As we're following it, Franck whispers, "'Request an audience', really?"

"When in Rome."

The staircase looks so much like old wood that I'm actually surprised that the steps don't creak under the weight of me and my suit. One day maybe I'll try and visit a real version of one of these places, back on Earth. There's nothing like the old world.

At the halfway landing, where the staircase splits in two, I point left. "You go that way, I'll go this way."

Franck turns within his helmet, trying to see upstairs. "You think there might be trouble?"

"Nah. Just thought it'd be fun. Race you."

I scoot past the aye-aye to dash up the right-hand flight of stairs. Franck arrives at the top a few seconds after me. He tries to give me a stern look but I can see he enjoyed that as much as I did.

The aye-aye doesn't react at all, the spoilsport. It just goes straight to a pair of double doors that you'd swear were oak, bends as if to pull them open, though of course it doesn't have hands, and they swing open smoothly. Me and Franck walk on in.

It's a bedroom. The walls appear wood-panelled and on the high white ceiling there are sculpted concentric circles and, hanging from it, a huge chandelier. Other than a patterned folding screen in one corner of the room and a free-standing oval mirror, the only item of furniture is an enormous four-poster bed with frills hanging from its roof. The curtains are pulled aside.

In the bed is a man, and it doesn't take an Optic to figure out that he's Felix Ransome. He's sitting up with a tray-with-legs over his lap, and on the tray sits a silver teapot and a plate of toast.

"Good morning," he says, casual as you like. Kudos to him for looking so calm meeting strangers in his jim-jams. "To what do I owe the pleasure?"

I don't mind telling you I feel a bit silly standing here in my bulky suit. I flip the catch of my helmet, pull it off and drop it onto the foot of the bed.

"I'm new here," I say. "So I thought I'd come say hello. You know, neighbourly. Is that marmalade?"

Ransome grins. He must be in his mid-fifties, but the smile belongs to someone way younger.

I can feel Franck's eyes on me as I stroll over to pluck a slice of toast from Ransome's plate. I munch away, humming with approval while I do. It takes fucking *good*.

Ransome pours coffee into the cup and hands it to me. I gulp it down. Tastes real. I'm not sure I like it, but it gives me a zing right away.

"Would you like me to call for more?" Ransome says, glancing at Franck.

Franck shakes his head frantically. "No, no. Thank you, sir. I apologise for interrupting you so early in the day."

I roll my eyes. It must be noon at least.

"It's always a pleasure to meet new people," Ransome says. He tucks his legs so they're free of the lap tray, then rolls over to the side of the bed, which takes a couple of seconds because it's so wide. He disappears behind the folding screen for a moment – on the folding screen is a tapestry showing a hunting party, and while it's quite pretty I don't approve of that sort of thing, for the record – then reappears wearing a crimson dressing gown and slippers. He's a class act.

He waits for me to say something, expectant but not hurried.

"I'm an Optic," I say. "Sent on behalf of Sagacity."

"Lovely."

"I'm investigating a death, over at Tharsis Caraway. Suspicious circumstances, I suppose you could say. A man named Jerem Ferrer."

I watch him carefully. There's no sign of recognition.

"I've been here the whole time," Ransome says, holding up both his hands, meaning *I'm innocent.*

"But she didn't tell you when this happened," Franck says.

Ransome giggles. "It wouldn't matter. I'm *always* here the whole time. This building is my home, my office and my hobby, all rolled into one."

"You never go outside?" I can't hide the pity from my voice.

He shakes his head. "Agoraphobia, you might call it. Or cowardice."

"Surely into the grounds, though?"

"No. There are cameras installed along the driveway, in the orchard, the herb garden, above the maze. I can see how it's all looking, and the effect it has on visitors like yourselves."

There's an upturn to the end of his statement – he's looking for approval. I'm happy to give it. "It's brilliant," I say, meaning it. "You're a talented fellow."

His shoulders bunch up with the excitement of a child. "Come, come and look."

He leads us out of the bedroom and through a smaller door on the carpeted landing. Inside are a few comfortable-looking armchairs facing a wall of screens, on which I can see views of every angle of the manor, including images of lush gardens. I peer at a feed showing a series of fountains in a long shallow pool.

"It's the only obstacle I can't quite overcome," Ransome says sadly. "What looks like water's actually solid. I tried installing projectors to simulate movement upon the surface, but it looked awfully tacky. I'll be honest, that problem was the reason for abandoning my old coastal residence." He turns to tap at a map on the wall, which shows several quadrants of the Martian landscape. The area he's pointing at has been drawn over with black pen, making a jagged line.

"The coast?" I say. My throat's gone dry. Franck looks over at me but I ignore him.

"It was a first attempt, by my predecessors," Ransome says airily.

"Can I see it?"

"I'm afraid I don't have a camera feed. I did once, but increasingly I found it made me sad to see it." He notices my disappointment. "Here, I must have a picture somewhere." He pulls at the drawers of a filing cabinet beside the armchairs, rummages through the hanging folders, pulls one out. "Just a schematic."

The paper shakes when I hold it. I wish Franck would stop staring at me.

The architect's drawing is full of perpendicular lines that obscure the image itself, but through the mesh I can see the seaside town. A hotel, tall seafront buildings, a pier. And hanging above it all is a long, high wave, curled at its top, just on the cusp of cresting.

It hasn't so much as crossed my mind for at least a decade. The image must have been buried somewhere in the back of my head.

I hand the paper back to Ransome, gripping my wrist with my other hand to keep it steady.

"Are you quite all right?" he says. Then, either because he's being delicate or because he's bad at reading people, he carries on. "It was a monstrosity. Just hanging there. It didn't look like liquid, only a wall. I could have had it pushed over and either started again or just opted for a less grandiose approach. But if you can't build water, what's the use of a seaside residence? So shifting towards landlocked rurality seemed the sensible option."

I suppose he's right. If something isn't working, get the hell out.

And I'm guessing this building was once intended to be a fancy hotel, or maybe to be hired out for corporate groups on a jolly from Earth. Given that there's not much call for that, why leave it unoccupied? Though I can't help but think of the residents of Tharsis Caraway, all trained up in hospitality professions. They'd go crazy for a place like this.

I stumble out of the viewing room and onto the landing. Franck and Ransome follow me out and watch me with their arms folded. They're actually quite similar-looking, apart from their outfits. Town mouse and country mouse.

I give my throat a good clear out. "Brass tacks, Mr Ransome. My investigation hinges on two things: whether your aye-ayes are capable of murder, and whether anyone might have any reason to want Jerem Ferrer dead."

He smiles. "One of those is easy to answer. An aye-aye could never cause harm."

I could inform him that Ai383 was modelled on his brain pattern. Instead I decide to watch him, to see whether they share any mannerisms. "And the second?"

"It's difficult to say. Or at least, it's difficult for me to say. I have no earthly idea who Jerem Ferrer might be."

I look to Franck.

Franck says, "He was a research scientist working solo at Tharsis Caraway. He specialised in the Martian crabs."

Ransome's eyebrows rise. "Really? How interesting. And what did he discover?"

"We don't know, sir," Franck replies.

"You must have approved the funding personally," I say.

Ransome waves a hand. "Indeed, that may be true. And if I were approached with such a request today, I would certainly offer my approval once again. Understanding the Martians is the only true and worthy occupation, wouldn't you agree?"

I look at Franck. I bet we're both thinking the same thing: if so, why is he spending all his time painting a fake country manor?

"So, to be clear, you didn't know Jerem Ferrer?" I say.

"I only wish I had," Ransome replies. "He sounds like a fascinating fellow."

"Can you think of anybody who might oppose him or his work?"

Ransome laughs softly. "'Anybody' seems the right word. We all have complicated relationships with the Martians, isn't that so?"

"How do you mean?"

"Apologies. Perhaps my reference is oblique to anybody not residing here. In short, the native Martians are successful citizens of this planet, whereas we humans are not. They thrive. They are not compelled to stumble around in oxygen suits. They are aloof to the economy, whether it is growing or failing."

"And yet they *are* the economy. Or were."

He shrugs. "It was only ever a blink of the eye. The diamond trade was no more than a short-term fix."

"And the long term?"

Ransome gestures at the walls around us. "The original plan remains unchanged. This place, and the spas and baths of the Daisychains resort, even the failed seafront. In short, tourism. People would come – from Earth, I mean – if only there was a compelling reason."

"I've just come from Earth. Believe me, it's not in great shape, financially."

He raises an eyebrow. "And you think that's what prevents people spending their hard-earned money on holidays?" He doesn't wait for an answer. "If anything, it makes it more likely. No, the issue is one of public perception. I've seen the Earth media feeds. The only footage of Mars ever shown is of barren desert, ruined structures. It's a narrative of a failed experiment."

I keep my mouth shut. I mean, what part of that description *isn't* the truth?

"So we need a breakthrough," Ransome says. "And once the first Earth citizens are convinced to visit, we would build more facilities, and then more people would come. Tourism would revive the economy, which would result in the arrival of more colonists, and so on and so on."

I decide to play along. "If it's not finances, what exactly do you think is stopping them, right now?"

"The storms, for one, but that obstacle is surmountable. The answer must be sand walls surrounding residential areas, higher than any yet built. Given appropriate funding, though more than Sandcastle has at its disposal, it would be child's play. But the bigger prize is the secret held by the native Martians."

Franck scrunches up his nose. He's thinking that all the crabs hold are worthless diamonds.

"You mean the ability to survive out there," I say.

Ransome nods. "Nobody in their right mind would spend their savings on a holiday which requires them to wear a bulky spacesuit for the duration."

I can think of a hundred other reasons why they wouldn't. It wouldn't be kind to list them to Ransome. Instead, I say, "Coincidentally, the Martians' innate abilities were very much what Jerem Ferrer was interested in, too."

He blinks. "Well there you go, then. That explains why I approved his funding." He draws himself up to his full height, which isn't much. "Have you slept yet? Have you had the dream?"

"Yes. The storm."

"It's another of my interests. Come this way. You'll like this."

Thirteen

Franck shoots me a look but I just shrug as Ransome scurries downstairs. You know me. I follow every lead, no matter what.

"I spend as much time as possible in bed," Ransome says over his shoulder as he dashes ahead. Me and Franck are like movie monsters, our heavy boots clomping after him. "Sleeping often feels like the optimum research method, in a curious way."

We're back in the lobby. Ransome strides to a tall pair of doors that look as if they must lead into a dining room or some other public room. If this was a murder mystery, the body would probably be in there.

I hope there isn't a body, though. One's plenty.

Ransome pulls the door open with a flourish, and I wonder if he's biting his tongue to stop himself from calling out 'Ta-da!'

The first things I notice are the sculptors, scooting around the enormous, high-ceilinged hall, their grimy suction funnels outstretched. No, actually, they're the second things. The first thing I notice is the dust. Franck actually coughs like he's choking, which must just be some unconscious reaction because of course his air supply's self-contained. I wish I hadn't left my helmet on Ransome's bed. When I get closer to him I see he's pulled a white mask out of his dressing-gown pocket, and he's covering his mouth and nose. Caramel-coloured dust is already beginning to collect on his shoulders like dandruff, and its static charge is making it stick to my gloves. He hands me a mask.

Ransome's voice is muffled when he says, "What do you think?"

He needs a cleaner, is what I think. There's already dust spilling out onto the tiled mosaic in the lobby. I squint to look at the bulbous shapes that are only now becoming visible – until now I'd taken them to be bulky columns holding up the ceiling.

The routes the sculptors are taking carefully avoid these big structures. The ones nearest to me are tricky to distinguish from the dust, because they're sculpted to *look* like dust — they're shaped like plumes and mushroom clouds, although they're solid and unmoving. Some look to be springing up from the floor, but others protrude from the walls. They're skilfully built, and many of them have spindly bases and end up resembling fat cauliflowers, but with no signs of teetering or fragility. I look beyond them and then I realise I can't properly make out the back wall of the hall, a hundred feet away. It looks like the wall of a cave, rough and irregular.

"Come," Ransome says, and we follow him, slow as sleepwalkers.

In fact, 'sleepwalking' feels like the right word. Because once I've passed the plume columns, I realise what these sculptors have been working so hard to build. I've been approaching it along one wall dotted with protrusions, but now I edge into the centre of the hall, careful not to knock anything with my suit pack, until I'm in the right position.

Because I've *seen* this. I saw it last night, while I was lying beside Hazel in her bed. I was standing stock still, not able to move, much as I am now, staring at *this* with my mouth hanging open.

It's the dust storm from my dream. The twisted shapes, painted tornadoes frozen in place, extend along the walls beyond where I'm standing, like arms ready to wrap around me. The same thing on the roof, but some trick of perspective makes it look as though the clouds go up forever, as opposed to stopping at the ceiling. And in front of me is a pit, or a dark window. There's a suggestion of constant motion even though I know nothing's moving in there at all. The sense of falling into it, downwards and upwards at the same time.

I stagger and Ransome takes my elbow — he's strong for someone so small.

"I —" I say, which is maybe all there is to say.

There's a thud beside me. Franck's dropped to his knees. He's pointing at the painted vortex.

His voice is tinny coming from his helmet speaker. Croaky, too. "It's perfect."

And it is. It's perfect. And not just a perfect recreation. Even though it isn't moving, even though the colours don't shift like they did in my dream, and the air's still dancing with everyday, orange dust spat out by the sculptors, it feels perfect because it prods at the same sensation inside me, that sense of somebody reaching into my belly and pulling something out that's *mine*, that's *me*, and more me than anything anyone's ever shown me before.

"You made this?" I say, and I'm so quiet that I'm surprised anyone notices.

"Together," Ransome replies, pointing at the half-dozen sculptors in turn.

"What does it mean?" Franck says in a shaky voice. I think he might be crying.

Ransome takes the mask away from his face. He looks tired suddenly. "That's one question I can't answer. I'm not even sure I'm trying to answer any questions. I just can't bear the thought that this is only available during sleep, or that —" He hesitates. "Or that that it might one day just stop, that it might go away."

I'm feeling dizzy suddenly. I don't *do* this — I don't get overwhelmed. I back away, then turn and stumble through the forest of sand plumes.

The other two catch up with me in the lobby, where I'm bent double and retching into my white mask. Franck tries to rub my back, but my suit's so bulky I can see it but can't feel it. I manage a smile and wave a hand weakly at the doors. Ransome closes them and I can breathe again.

"Can I offer you some water?" Ransome says, beckoning to an aye-aye that slides out from the shadows beyond the staircase.

I shake my head. "I'm good." I hand him my little mask and to his credit he doesn't even glance at the coffee-coloured spit pooling inside it, and just pops it into his pocket.

"How did you do it?" I ask. "How did you communicate it to the sculptors? I mean your..." I think about the right word for what we've all been looking at. "Vision."

The aye-aye's still padding towards us. Ransome waits for it to come close, then he points at the closed doors. "Aye-aye one-sixteen. That sculpture we've been building in the east hall. Have you seen such a thing before?"

The aye-aye bows respectfully. "Yes."

"Where?"

"Nocturnal standby."

"Or to state it in more prosaic terms, in your dreams?"

"Yes."

The aye-aye turns to look at the door. Its head tilts just a little, as if it's trying to look through the slit where the doors join, or more likely picturing what's behind them.

"It's the same with the sculptors," Ransome says. "They share a network, so it's hardly a surprise that they might share an outlook. But quite how these dreams are introduced to them is a mystery, and no less a mystery is why they experience the same dream that we colonists enjoy every evening. But all I can say is that I'm glad. The more the merrier."

Franck exhales. "So it's a collaboration, that sculpture? You're all providing input?"

"I suppose you could say I'm the foreman. But no more than that. I've given the go-ahead, ultimately, and I can allow myself some credit for that. But yes. We're a team. That's how I like it. Every morning and late every afternoon, the entire household congregates in the east hall and we pay our respects. It's rather moving."

It should sound stupid, I know. But I can't argue with any of it. And stranger still, I'm envious.

Ransome frowns when I shake my head, but I'm only doing it to clear my thoughts.

"Hold on," I say. "Franck, you checked over Ferrer's suit, right?"

Franck looks startled, like the vision of the storm made him forget about the case. "Yes, of course."

"And there were no records of Ferrer's activity?"

"It's an old suit. It doesn't have any recording functionality."

"Fine. And aye-aye three-eight-three's memory was wiped by the reset. But what about the others?"

Franck's eyes move to Ransome's aye-aye which is standing patiently, waiting for instructions. His eyes get wider.

"The cloud," he says softly, and Ransome flinches, and I know we're all thinking again about the dust storms in our dreams. "I mean the network."

Ransome blinks in confusion as I reach out to shake him by the hand.

"It's been an absolute pleasure," I say, "but we must dash back to Tharsis Caraway. I hope we'll cross paths again."

He's still blinking rapidly as I stride over to the airlock, and he's still blinking when I spin and race back upstairs and then down again, muttering about leaving my helmet on his bed. He waves when I pass him again, and his hand's resting on the handle of the door to the east hall that contains his storm sculpture, and I already feel sad that we didn't get to spend more time in there, and I wish that Franck and I didn't have a job to do.

Fourteen

"This is all of them? Other than her?" I point at Ai383, who's still powered down and hanging from the metal struts in her locker. Her loose body looks really sad.

Franck walks along the row of aye-ayes in the centre of the workshop. They're identical, all standing erect, side by side, their short limbs hanging at their sides. Docile.

"Twelve, thirteen," he says. Then he looks up, still counting. "I think there are maybe four missing."

"'Maybe'?"

He looks sheepish. "They're not used for all that much these days. It might sound silly, but they're pretty much free to come and go. Probably one or two are elsewhere in the base somewhere, or maybe helping out at the chapel."

I look at the row of blank faces. They're as smooth as anything the sculptors could produce.

"Can I speak to them all at once?" I say.

Franck shrugs. "I've never tried."

"Aye-aye units?" I say. "I'm addressing each and every one of you. Do you understand?"

"Yes." It's a queasy effect, the voices coming from all around. I'm sure they're speaking in sync but the acoustics of the large workshop gives the effect of a slight lag.

"I need you to tell me about aye-aye three-eight-three. Please search your records for any trace of her activity."

Silence.

"Have you found anything?"

"Yes." Again, it sounds like a single voice coming from all around, or as if it's inside my head.

"I should warn you," Franck says to me, "Caraway's cloud is antiquated, and the base walls are thick. While the aye-ayes are technically capable of communicating on the same network, their ability to speak to one another, or transfer data, if you like, is severely limited. We have a range of a couple of hundred metres, at best."

"Noted. And when was it that you found Ferrer dead? The fifteenth?"

"Fourteenth." He gives me a funny look. I knew it was the fourteenth, though. It's always worth keeping sidekicks on their toes.

"Starting from this end —" I point to the aye-aye at the left of the row. "State the most recent date of your records relating to three-eight-three."

The first aye-aye says calmly, "Thursday the tenth of March."

The next says, "Wednesday the ninth of March."

They all name dates in turn. I see Franck raise his eyebrows as two of them in a row say, "Monday the fourteenth of March."

I point at those two. "Step forward, would you? State your IDs."

They obey. The first says, "Two-nine-one." The second: "Three-zero-eight."

"Okay. Two-nine-one. Where were you when you recorded three-eight-three's activities?"

"In kitchen number eleven."

"And the same question for you, three-zero-eight."

"Here, in the workshop."

I frown, look around, try to picture the layout of the base. Ferrer's lab is an external construction, only connected to Tharsis Caraway by corridor. I hadn't realised it, but that corridor must bend around so that the lab's close to where we're standing now, otherwise the signal wouldn't have made it.

"Was any other aye-aye present in the workshop at the time? Whether shut down or operational?"

"No," Ai308 replies.

"And did you receive any data from any other aye-aye at the same time? That's a question for both of you."

"No," they both reply together.

I take a deep breath. "That's a relief. Makes things a whole lot simpler. So, what have you got?"

They don't say anything.

"Three-zero-eight. What's the nature of your most recent record?"

"A block series of commands from a human operator, relayed verbally and executed in sequential order by aye-aye three-eight-three."

"What kind of actions? Broadly speaking."

"Pick up barrier. Provide temporary obstacle to obstruct forward movement of native Martian lifeform. Angle lamp. Operate lamp."

I puff out my cheeks. "And that was your final record? Why did the connection terminate?"

"Yes. I was summoned from the workshop. I left to respond to a call from a resident on the fifth floor."

To the other aye-aye I say, "And now you. Please, tell me your most recent record."

Ai291 replies, "I cannot state my most recent record."

I narrow my eyes. "Can't, or won't?"

The aye-aye watches me blankly. "My most recent record of aye-aye three-eight-three is video footage. It is a captured echo of that unit's own visual feed."

Franck and I exchange looks.

"And this was on the fourteenth of March… How long is it?"

"Thirty-five seconds."

"And what's the timestamp at its end point?"

"Eleven-sixteen a.m."

"Franck – what time did you receive the distress call?"

His face is twitchy with excitement. "Eleven-sixteen."

Fifteen

I can see Ai383's stubby limbs in front of me. Even though the monitor's small and the feed is crackling with static, my face is close enough to the screen that for a second the effect fools me, and I can almost believe those handless limbs are mine.

I'm looking down at one of the crabs on the floor of Ferrer's lab – the airless part of the Venn diagram. It skitters around a bit within an enclosure formed from two transparent barriers placed against the wall. Light is shining from my arm stub, illuminating the Martian and casting a Nosferatu shadow on the rough wall. I'm low to the ground. I think maybe I'm crouching.

"Where's Ferrer?" Franck says beside me. His head's touching mine as we both peer at the monitor. He smells a bit fusty and a bit like sweets.

With each second that passes my heart sinks a bit more. Perhaps this is all the footage will show: three-eight-three staring at a crab. It's not enough to prove or disprove her guilt. Anything could be happening to Ferrer right at this moment.

I exhale with relief as the crab disappears from view. Ai383 is turning around, and rising at the same time. I squint to examine the details as the aye-aye's gaze sweeps over the rough sand walls. There's the suggestion of a curve towards the hole in the domed roof, which I can't quite see. There's a diagonal scrape across the surface of the wall.

Then there's Ferrer. He's wearing his suit. His helmet has a faded smiley-face sticker on the bottom right – maybe he once had a sense of humour. There's a weird look on his face and his right arm's outstretched towards me, pointing with his index finger. It's creepy seeing him alive, partly because until now I've only known him as a corpse on a kitchen island, and partly his eyes look quite like Hazel's.

"What's he saying?" I whisper.

Franck makes a noncommittal noise.

Ferrer's lips are moving but there's no audio to the recording, or at least nothing useful. The monitor speakers are definitely working, as was Ai383's audio recording equipment, because I can hear muffling bumping sounds. The audio must be corrupted.

Ferrer pulls back his outstretched hand. What's that expression on his face? It'd be hard to describe it as full-on panic, but it's not far off.

He indicates his helmet. Both his hands are pointing at his head. He's saying something but there's still no audio.

Three-eight-three watches, and so do I.

Ferrer keeps pointing, moving his hands back and forth for emphasis. Is that anger?

Then I see my arms. Three-eight-three's arms. Both of them lifting up towards Ferrer's head, either side of his helmet.

The stubs glow blue.

Ferrer's expression changes completely as his head turns within his helmet, looking to either side at the blue stubs. Then his head turns faster – he's shaking it frantically. His lips work soundlessly.

Then the arm stubs twist and so does the helmet. I can see a gap widening at its base. It's coming off.

Ferrer's eyes are wild. Suddenly a sound comes through the speakers, so abruptly that I almost topple backwards off my stool. It isn't a word, just a squeal of static.

Then the video feed cuts off.

Sixteen

I'm stumbling through the corridors again. It's early and nobody else is up.

I wish I hadn't decided to spend the night alone. My room was cold and the only choices of lamp settings were too dim or too bright. I haven't slept in total blackness since I was a kid.

Those dreams.

The joy was still there, but it was all muddled. I couldn't see them, but I was sure Felix Ransome and Franck were standing at my side. Maybe Hazel, and others, too, but I couldn't turn to look. I just stared at the whirling red dust as it edged closer, or perhaps I was skidding towards it, but either way it was ready to envelop me, and my feelings about the prospect were more mixed than you'd expect.

And I couldn't breathe.

I've had sleep apnoea since I was little – pauses in my breathing while I'm asleep. It was never too serious but it gave my folks a scare, more than once. I always liked to think that my condition was the reason for them sending me away from Mars. Safer on Earth, where there were actual doctors rather than what people generously called 'medics'. I don't know. I was young. And they're dead, so I can't ask.

And who knows how long I stopped breathing for, in my sleep last night. One thing's reassuring: it woke me up. I burst out from under the sheets as if they were the surface of a lake, clutching at my throat.

I saw a face hanging in front of me. A hallucination.

It was Jerem Ferrer. His eyes bulging, his cheeks slack, his mouth a big O with the realisation that he was already asphyxiating.

I don't know where I'm heading, and even though my stomach's grumbling with hunger, my feet take me down to the cargo bay.

Our AkTrak trundler's right where we parked it yesterday.

Its door swings open the moment I touch it – my requisition must still apply. I grab my suit from the peg on the wall, shuffle into it. I wish I'd had a shower, and that I hadn't slept in my clothes. I tell myself that once this case is done and dusted I'll clean up my act. Maybe even buy a flat. If I had a home, I might actually feel like hanging around there every so often, rather than just dotting from hotel to hotel working cases. I've got a shit-ton of savings. I could get one of those baths with animal claws for feet.

Once I'm outside, the trundler carves a gulley into the dust that's settled into new humps overnight. It feels good to be in control. I steer from side to side so that the caterpillar tracks bump against the more established heaps bordering the nominal track, which are the results of the sculptors' clearing long ago. In them I can see layers, like a cross-section of sedimentary rock; loose dust at the top, then harder regolith – light in colour and so brittle that flakes come free immediately – and underneath that, dark as chocolate.

Seventeen

The place was just a chapel when I was a kid. It always seemed strange, being out on its own in the dunes. The sand barrier surrounding it was barely taller than the little spire, but the storms never seemed to cause the building any damage. Mum said it was cleverly located, because the winds whipped along the smooth plains of Chryse basin but then ended up funnelled along the outflow channels formed by floods billions of years ago. Dad said it was divine intervention.

The little sign outside the building still describes the place as a chapel – the Chapel of Oxia Palus and Our Father, just like it was before – but that's a joke. It's *enormous*. Even though the walls are plain, with no hint of the Gothic like you'd find in churches back home, standing before it makes me ask myself the same question as when I visited the Sagrada Familia in Barcelona. And the question is: *where the hell are they getting the money for all this?*

I pull up beside a huge scrum of other trundlers – most of them much larger than mine, with room for dozens of passengers inside – and there also are a few fleets of AkTraks tethered together on connecting rods, like a bus made of individual cars. People are still emerging from a few of the vehicles. Their suits look shabby and patched, barely safe. I'm wondering what they make of the scale of the chapel. I know I'd be pissed off.

I queue up behind the others. Even though the airlock's big, with room for ten at a time, it still takes several minutes before I'm inside. It's dark and the room beyond is just a vestibule. The people ahead of me shrug off their suits and helmets and put them onto wide trays, then the trays move away, carried off by adapted sculptor robots. I feel a weird flash of outrage at them being demoted to valets. None of the churchgoers seem concerned about whether they'll end up with the same suits when they leave, but then again the suits all look equally crappy. I wonder what their intended professions were due to be, when the tourists arrived. Waiters, tour guides, clowns, escorts, life guards.

I pull off my suit and, when nobody's looking, I shove it in a corner and then drag a free-standing whiteboard across to hide it. I hesitate for a moment, then pull my pistol from my suit and transfer it to the waist pouch of my jeans. In neat handwriting on the whiteboard is a Bible passage: *The Lord is good, a stronghold in the day of trouble; he knows those who take refuge in him.*

When I head into the main atrium of the chapel, the difference in sound quality feels almost like a change in atmospheric pressure. I grab onto the back of a pew to stop myself from veering to one side – the interior's so large that I feel kind of adrift, as if I might float away from the floor. It's dim and I can only just make out the high ceiling, which seems miles away. The building's been designed to impress its congregation with scale rather than artistic flourishes – there are no patterns or curlicues or paintings, only plain, slanted, sand-sculpted blocks, like we're in an enormous Lego house.

There must be two hundred people in here – some of them must have travelled from bases other than Caraway – but you'd never know. It's quiet as a grave.

People get all fidgety as us newcomers shuffle into the back pews. Looks like the service is just about to begin.

In the darkness my dream comes back to me. The storm, and Ferrer's ghostly face. I catch myself thinking that maybe divine guidance might be some comfort right now.

But I still feel a fool for finding myself here this morning. It's nothing to do with the case, and it shows I'm weak.

I blink as bright lights puncture the gloom. Above me is a white beam with dust dancing in it, like the projection in retro cinemas which, when I was a kid, I'd always try to grab when the film started. It's shining onto the far wall, which seems a thousand miles away. The bulb must be good. The plain wall that the congregation is facing isn't a plain wall any more. Now there's a stained-glass window that must be sixty feet tall and forty wide, and it's so convincing that it seems weird that it wasn't already illuminated when the congregation arrived, rather than spoil the illusion by turning it on abruptly like this. Most of the window's filled with big patches of colour, with dark and light blue to represent the sky, vivid green at the bottom for grass, but I can also see figures. They're all working – tilling earth, sowing seeds, bending into wells. To anyone born here on Mars, this sort of thing must seem like science fiction.

Organ music starts to play. I look around but can't see any speakers. There couldn't be a real organ here, could there? The congregation rise so I figure I'd better do the same. They all start singing. I don't know the song, and I don't even bother to mouth words. I have my limits.

Between the heads of the people in the next row I see somebody walk onto the podium beneath the stained-glass window. He looks tiny against the scale of the chapel, and he's dressed in a plain black robe. He's bald and maybe in his sixties, but even from here at the back I can see that there's youth in his eyes, an energy. He strides to the centre of the podium and grips either side of a plain lectern.

"Friends," he says. His voice carries throughout the space perfectly, without seeming to be amplified. "Welcome to you all, whether this chapel is familiar or new to you, and whether you are familiar or new to us."

Maybe somebody clocked me on the way in. Maybe the Reverend was watching goings-on in the vestibule remotely, noticing me stash my suit, marking me out as different.

But he isn't looking my way. I follow the direction of his gaze, over to the left-hand side at the back of the hall.

"Sit," the Reverend says, and everybody does. But I stand for a moment longer to see a group of figures on three consecutive rows, tucked away in the shadows of an overhang.

They're aye-ayes, perhaps twenty of them. They take their places on the pews and raise their blank faces to the podium.

Well, that's weird.

"We will begin as we always begin," the Reverend says, gazing around at the congregation, all smugness. "With a moment's silence. Take this time to retreat to somewhere within yourself. Reach your hands out towards our dream. We will share it together."

Heads nod forward and stay there. I look over at the aye-ayes – they're doing it too. Only me and the Reverend are still looking around. He frowns at me and I give a thumbs-up.

After thirty seconds, he announces, "Thank you, friends. It feels good to share, does it not? And it is meaningful, too. We all have our concerns, our worries, our fears. And it is tempting to consider this chapel a safe place from the storm and a shadow from the heat, as is described in Isaiah. Yes, we are safe in his shelter. Yes, this is a refuge. But we should not consider our dream, our storm, a malign symbol. We should embrace it. It is beautiful – we can all agree on that. Awesome, yes. Perhaps even terrifying, as true beauty often can be. But what does it represent?"

The heads are up now, all eyes on him. Breaths are held and necks craned.

The Reverend continues, "The storm represents our hardship, my friends. From Psalm one-oh-seven: 'Yet when they cried out to the Lord in their trouble, the Lord brought them out of their distress. He calmed the storm and its waves quieted down. So they rejoiced that the waves became quiet, and he led them to their desired haven'." He pauses, letting his words ring. "It is not for me to describe our desired haven, as each of us will harbour a different image of it – a city, a Garden of Eden." His eyes flick up, as if he's trying to direct our attention subtly to the pastoral images in the stained-glass window behind him. "But we can all identify with the words 'distress' and 'trouble'. And we all witness the storm, the *true* storm, every night. And so the message is clear. We must cry out to the Lord in our trouble."

There's fidgeting around me. At first I think it's boredom and I'm surprised, but then I realise it's not that. It's anticipation.

"Friends," the Reverend says, raising his voice. "Let us cry out to the Lord in our trouble. Now."

I flinch at the first voice.

"I don't know where I'm —" a woman begins, but then she's drowned out by somebody in the row in front of me, a man, who says, "I think I have —" but then he's also overwhelmed by more voices, more and more. I realise that everyone around me is speaking, loudly, their chins raised to project their complaints and questions into the empty air of the enormous hall. I rise from my seat a bit to see over the heads. The entire congregation is pleading with the Reverend, or the chapel, or God. While I can't hear any of the aye-ayes to my left, their heads are tilted up too and I'm certain they're doing the same.

You'll be glad to know that the thought doesn't even cross my mind to join in. I may be haunted by the storm, and Jerem Ferrer, and maybe my parents too, but this isn't the way to come to terms with it all.

The Reverend allows the moaning and muttering to go on for more than a minute. Then he raises his hands. The voices peter out bit by bit, and he nods indulgently, without a hint of hurry.

When it's all silent again, he says, "And therein lies the problem, my friends. I hear your voices. I certainly hear your volume!" He chuckles like he's told a joke, and there's a rippled echo of his laughter all around. "And yet I cannot understand your precise distress, your trouble. It is a matter of patience, of course. I can, and I will, hear each and every one of your concerns, at a time of your choosing. I am at your disposal. But I can answer your concerns only to a limited degree. I am not your Lord. And so, the conclusion must be that it is a matter of language. This babble of voices may make itself heard, but from our ongoing blessed dream we must conclude that it is not yet *understood*. But we will, and we must, try."

The Reverend's body loosens, and it's only now that I realise just how rigid he's been. He shakes his arms like he's limbering up for a run.

"Phew!" he says, wiping his forehead. "Intense stuff, huh?"

There's more laughter from all the sycophants around me.

"Everything I've said may be true," he continues, "but that doesn't mean we can't afford ourselves a little fun all the same. Am I right?"

A murmur of approval.

"I said, am I right?"

A hearty "Yes," and a few cautious whoops.

"Okay! So let's treat ourselves to another song."

The organ starts up again and everybody gets to their feet, already singing their bloody hearts out. It's another one I've never heard. I keep my lips pressed tight together as I stare at the Reverend over people's heads. He's watching me, too.

Eighteen

After the service I edge to one side of the pew and let the others filter out into the vestibule. It takes forever for the queues to thin out – even if each member of the congregation grabs any suit rather than looking for the one they came in, it still takes a while to put them on – and while people are waiting they pass their wristbands over a donation scanner beside the door. Every penny helps to keep a place this size properly maintained.

As I'd expected, the aye-ayes hang back too. They know their place. I glance over at the podium before heading over to them. When he finished speaking the Reverend disappeared into a back room and hasn't shown up again.

"Can I speak to you for a moment?" I ask, addressing the whole group of aye-ayes.

Their identical blank faces turn to me. If they had eyes instead of smooth pits, they'd be blinking in surprise.

I point at one of them at random. "What brings you here, if you don't mind me asking?"

"The sermon," it replies calmly.

"You enjoyed it?"

"I appreciated it."

It's an interesting choice of words, I suppose. I smile. "I've only been on Mars for a couple of days, but I had the dream both nights. You have it too, all of you?"

"Yes," they reply together.

"And do you think the Reverend's right? That it's a symbol of something?"

The first aye-aye says, "All communication involves symbolism."

"So you're certain it's communication, this shared dream of ours?"

"Yes," they say in unison.

"And might it be related to your brain pattern templates? Trace memories of your human donors?"

"I do not think so," the first aye-aye says.

Perhaps the aye-ayes are more startled by the dreams than anyone. They must appear like original, imaginative thoughts.

"And what do you think it might mean?"

At first they don't reply. Then, as one, they all say, "I do not know."

I look over my shoulder. There are only a handful of colonists still queuing. "I won't take up much more of your time. But I just wondered what you make of the Reverend. I'm guessing you approve of him in general?"

The first aye-aye replies, "Yes."

I tilt my head. "Is there anything else you can tell me? About your feelings about him? Sorry, not feelings. How about, um, observations."

"I appreciate Reverend Guillaume. He presents facts clearly and makes compelling cases for their interpretation. He is effective at communicating."

I nod. "So are you. Thank you for your time. I'm sure you have places you need to be."

Or maybe they don't. Maybe they're all essentially free operators these days, like the aye-ayes on Tharsis Caraway. Perhaps some of these actually *are* the missing aye-ayes from Caraway, redundant now that human colonists are desperate to avoid finding themselves unoccupied. To be honest, I don't much care. Aye-ayes deserve a bit of freedom, and it feels cruel to hold them up by pestering them with questions. They're simple folk and I like them.

I wave them goodbye and plod up the central aisle. When I reach the podium I hop up onto it rather than using the steps, then I turn and put both my hands on the lectern just as Reverend Guillaume did. Even though the podium's not all that high up, I can imagine how powerful he must feel, standing here and looking down at all those upturned faces.

I have to duck to go through the doorway the Reverend entered. The room is narrower than I'd expected, and I figure there must be other back rooms alongside it, entered from elsewhere.

Guillaume is sitting in a wing-backed armchair behind a big old desk that faces the door. Looks like mahogany, though it must be painted sand. His head's bent to a screen embedded into the surface of the desk, and as I get closer I see beige, creased pages – these must be scans of an old Bible, rather than a transcription.

He looks up. "Welcome. I thought you might make your way back here. Please, sit."

I take one of the two armchairs on the opposite side of the desk to him. It's pretty comfy and I have to remind myself not to sink into it. The chairs and the desk aren't the only displays of excess in the study. On the right-hand wall is a painted mural of the Martian landscape – caramel dunes and a still, purplish night sky with pinprick stars. The more I look, the more details I notice: I can even see tracks winding through the dunes, all of which are different shapes and sizes. No sign of storms or sculptors, but even so, whoever created this had talent.

A wide tapestry hangs on the opposite wall. It shows the Flood – the waves rushing from the right, overwhelming fields and tiny stragglers. On the left is the ark, just beginning to bob as the water reaches its hull. Noah, his family and the animals are leaning over the side, ambiguous little smirks on all their faces.

You can't sand-sculpt a tapestry. This must have been smuggled in from Earth. It couldn't have been cheap.

When I turn back to Guillaume he's examining the tapestry too. Then he presses himself back into his chair and takes a deep breath. "So. Tell me your tale."

I raise an eyebrow. "Is this a confession?"

"If you like. Do you have something you'd like to confess?"

94

I chew that over for a moment. "Not really."

So now we're just looking at each other. I don't trust religious people and I'm certain it shows. "Your sermon seemed to go down well. I spoke to some of your congregation. Some of the aye-ayes."

He smiles. "It's encouraging, isn't it? That I'm able to speak to their concerns as well as the colonists."

"You feel that you can help them?"

He spreads his hands. "That's not for me to say. But they keep coming, week after week. As I say: encouraging."

"And do they confess?"

"I wouldn't be so bold as to call it that. I wouldn't presume to say that they're capable of sin."

He's watching me carefully. Maybe he sees some small reaction – a tell – that shows I'm getting more interested.

"Why do you say that?" I say. "Sin?"

"Only because that's what preoccupies the thoughts of so many of us."

"But not the aye-ayes?" When he doesn't reply, I say, "So then what do they talk about in confession?"

Guillaume waves a hand to indicate the room we're in. "You must understand that 'confession' is a term I use through force of habit, and of course our chapel represents rather a muddle of the old religions. Anybody is welcome to join me in here, just as you have. Anybody is welcome to share their thoughts with me. It's just a chat. I'm good at chatting."

"And yet you haven't answered my question."

"The aye-ayes are hesitant. They talk about not fears so much as… this will sound melodramatic, but I want to say 'hauntings'. They're haunted by echoes of their human donors' memories, a phenomenon which is reasonably well-documented, though fascinating all the same. But they're haunted by their dreams of the storm, too. I suppose we all are."

I nod slowly. "And what you said out there, about the dreams representing some kind of instruction to speak to God. You believe that wholeheartedly?"

"It's one interpretation."

"It is. And another is duller than that – that the dream is a reflection of the barrenness of Mars, and the isolation. Or a more interesting interpretation – that it's a literal communication, with nothing divine about it. That it's the native Martians, trying to establish a framework of language to speak to us, humans and aye-ayes alike."

To my surprise, Guillaume doesn't protest. "All valid. All fascinating. All with implications." He pauses. "You haven't told me anything about yourself. Though I know that you're an Optic, and you arrived from Earth only recently."

"How do you know that?"

He laughs. "Don't worry. I'm not a Cardinal Richelieu type, with spies in every household. In my line of work you tend to pick up on clues. We're not so different, you and I."

I figure he can already see how much I dislike that idea, so I don't bother to say so.

"One also learns to select optimum lines of enquiry," he continues. "For example, I find myself wondering, do you have some link to Mars, other than your current occupation, whatever that may be?"

I stiffen. "I'm investigating the death of Jerem Ferrer, a research scientist working at Tharsis Caraway. It appears, at least at first glance, that his death could have been caused by an aye-aye."

Guillaume doesn't respond in any way.

I puff out my cheeks. In for a penny. "Yeah. And I was born here. Left when I was still a kid."

He nods. "And your parents?"

"They stayed. I was told – later – that they wanted a better life for me." I tell myself not to offload any more, but then I ignore my own instruction. "And if they knew that things were about to go south on Mars, that's fair enough. But if they *didn't* know that... Maybe they just wanted a better life for *them*."

I'm angry at myself for opening up to him. I wish Franck was here, or Hazel, or you.

Guillaume looks down at the screen embedded in his desk. "I have almost complete records here. I can find them."

He's already concluded that I don't know what happened to them. His deductive abilities are beginning to rile me up as much as the prodding at my memories. But still I crane my neck to watch as he taps and swipes at the screen. The Bible scan's replaced by folders, then a mass of text.

"Your name?"

"Abbey Oma. Abigail."

"Oma. Oma. Yes."

I grip the arms of the chair.

Guillaume hums as he scrolls through the list. Smug bastard.

"I see you," he says finally. "You left in eighty-six. Reason not stated."

"Uh-huh."

"Your parents were Richard and, let me see... Meryl."

"Yes. What does it say?"

He looks up. His expression is neutral. "I'm afraid they're no longer with us."

I know that. I *know* that. He's not telling me anything new. But my voice is tiny as I say, "When did they die?"

"Eighty-seven. No cause is recorded."

I can't speak. I can't anything.

"I'm sorry," Guillaume says. Then, after a few seconds, "Can I make you a cup of tea? Earl Grey? It was a gift that arrived with the final intake of colonists."

"No," I manage to say.

"Maybe something stronger."

"No." Not here, not right now. I *will* have something stronger, though, back at Caraway. You know me. I don't like to look back.

I rub at my face, avoiding my eyes because if I touch them I swear I'll cry and keep on crying.

"Right," I say. "Thanks for that. And now I have a question for you. Do you trust the aye-ayes?"

Guillaume feigns surprise at my mind being back on the job. "They're programmed to serve. Despite these glimpses into some fundamental characteristics underpinning them, they're lackeys by design. Aren't they?"

I shake my head, meaning *I ask the questions*. "Can you think of any reason why they might wish any of the colonists harm?"

"None," Guillaume says. Later, I'll have a good think about whether his answer was too quick.

"What about the crabs?"

"Why would the aye-ayes wish to harm the native Martians?"

"I'm asking you. No, hold on. Actually, I meant: might the crabs want to harm anyone else?"

My head's spinning. I'm not sure I know what I mean.

"These are all interesting hypotheses, Abigail. You're as much a theoretician as I am."

"No. I'm doing a job. I want to know whether…" I close my eyes, trying to recalibrate. "Whether aye-ayes are really conscious, or whether they're just suffering from some kind of illusion."

Guillaume's eyes glisten. Maybe he's offended by the idea.

"It's a fascinating idea, isn't it?" he says, leaning forward. "And yet even if that were the case, it would come back to the subject of my sermon, at least in terms of the implications of your suggestion, wouldn't it? It boils down to an ability to communicate. Would that there were a universal language in place of this Babel."

Something's rising up in my belly. I wonder if I'll be sick. The room feels too small and suddenly I wish I was out on the dunes.

"I have to go," I say.

Reverend Guillaume nods. "Let me say this, though. If an aye-aye killed this research scientist of yours, its motivation hardly matters, does it? Only that it was capable of murder."

It seems such an unreasonable statement, but what makes it worse is that at this precise moment I can't think of an argument against it. I stand up shakily.

"Thank you for your time," I say.

He nods, cheerful as ever. I turn and take a few steps before lurching to one side. I steady myself against the wall, accidentally tugging at the tapestry. I try to cover for my clumsiness by touching it as if I'm admiring it.

"It's very beautiful, isn't it?" Guillaume says behind me. "And it's a tonic to feel something not made of sand."

I'm too close to take in the image. I pass my fingers over the tapestry, feeling the bumps of individual threads. As well as the softness, it's oddly warm to the touch. It makes me think of stupid things. Jumpers and bodies and hugs.

I head out of the chapel without looking back.

Nineteen

I don't plug any coordinates into the dashboard of the trundler. I head east, only course-correcting to avoid chasms or when the computer bleeps to signal that the ground ahead might easily fall away.

Within a couple of hours I see landmarks I recognise. The buildings are in bad shape, with bits missing, windows open to the elements, but the skyline's still familiar. The ten-storey leisure complex, built in a hurry in response to the bigger and better Daisychains resort down south. The cafés, the shops selling tat. The Excelsior hotel overlooking the public square. To the north and south, curving towards each other with a relatively narrow gap between, are the sand-sculpted barriers built as protection against the storms. They're half the height they once were, and they're rounded at the top from wind erosion and lack of maintenance.

Directly ahead, identifying the location of the coastline before I can see it, is the wave.

I make a sort of *peep* sound as I squint up at it. The wave's utterly fucked, as badly eroded as the barriers, though in a couple of spots I can still see the upper fronds that were supposed to represent the foam on its crest. In other parts it looks like a seascape in profile rather than head-on; all humps and bumps rather than a single wave rising up above the town. I can't see a fleck of paint on it at all. I remember the exact shade of turquoise the wave used to be. Now it looks sickly like chewed toffee.

Felix Ransome was right. It never did look like liquid.

But it was *magnificent*.

I park on the seafront, get out, hold on to the spindly bar that runs along the shore, stare up at the wave.

When I was a kid I'd look up at it like this. I'd swear that I could hear the rushing sound of the water. Now all I can imagine is the thud it'd make if it came down, right now.

My stomach rumbles again. What kind of an adult forgets to eat?

I turn and then freeze.

There's somebody standing on the far side of the public square. No. *Two* somebodies.

The sunlight's in my eyes. My gloved fingers tap on my visor when I reach up instinctively to rub them. I squint.

They're gone.

No, no, no. I tell myself to get a grip.

There was nobody there. There's nobody here. At all. Just me and a mound of memories.

My parents are *not* here at the coast, I tell myself. They have *not* been waiting for me to return. They're long dead.

The intention was always to put a dome over this whole place, which would have turned the piazza into something usable, once people could step out of their suits. Outdoor cafés, a boules sandpit, kids with ice creams. The funding never showed up, so the piazza was only ever something to look at from inside the surrounding buildings. I remember a row of life-size figurines, designed by children and chosen by public vote: statues of family members, film stars from back home, invented monsters, aye-ayes, pets. The clods of dust upon the sculpted paving is what remains of them.

I plod across the piazza. My stomach growls.

I spin around.

Fuck.

There. Those two people again, gone now but only because they slipped into an alley between a café and an oxy-tank refill shop.

It was only a glimpse, but the suits looked odd. Not smooth and bulbous like most. Battered and blackened and angular.

Looters, is my opinion. There must be such people, in a place like this. I'd best leave them to their own devices, make clear I'm not here to spoil their fun.

I back away. The airlock door of the Excelsior Hotel is hanging open. Inside, sand covers the floor, the concierge desk and the armchairs lined up against the curved wall of the wide lobby, which is circular apart from the flat section of wall at the back, where the lift doors are.

It's calming to be inside, but my mind just starts racing off in another direction. The shape of the lobby makes me think of Ferrer's lab. The chamber in which Ai383 killed him.

Because that's a fact. Ai383 killed Ferrer.

After we'd watched the visual-feed footage ten times over, I froze the video at several points and extracted grabs. In the lab, me and Franck checked the stills against the walls of the chamber. Straight away, we were able to orient ourselves to the exact spot that Ai383 had stood, by comparing the marks on the walls. The same imperfections in the rough wall curving up to the roof hole. Franck had got excited about the long diagonal fissure in both the image and the wall before us, as if it indicated some kind of struggle. But I checked and it was obvious that it'd been made yonks ago, perhaps a glitch in the original template used by the sculptors that built it.

I'd stood where Jerem Ferrer had been standing when he died, and I'd looked up at the hole in the roof, staring at the circle of sky tinged with dusk like blood.

Nobody could have mistaken the chamber for one filled with air, least of all an aye-aye. Even if Ai383's oxygen sensors were knackered, she'd have been paralysed. I even checked all around the roof hole – if it'd ever been covered, even temporarily, there would have been marks to show where the lid was clamped on. The room *must* have been airless. But then Ai383 couldn't have plucked the helmet off Ferrer's head. Even if she were capable of making a mistake – even if Ferrer had demanded that she do it – she couldn't have murdered him.

Unless, of course, she could.

You can imagine the situation as well as I can. Right now, the corporate team at Sagacity are probably huddled up in their top-floor boardroom, shitting themselves. It isn't just the story that might get out. If an AI were proved capable of harming a human, then *all* of them are liabilities. All the household robots, the air-conditioning units, the digital valets, the waste-plant surveyors, the immunity bots.

It might all be fine. Or it might be a matter of time. And then it wouldn't be just a public relation issue, it'd be the real deal. At best, Sagacity would have to start over, scrapping all the tech and beginning again. At worst... a struggle, a battle, a war.

That's how they'll see it, anyway. Me, I'm just doing my job.

I grin as I approach the doors to the restaurant. They're vacuum-sealed – not as good as an airlock, but they'll do. It's dark inside and there's no power and no windows, so I heave a table over to prop open the door. I make my way around the chairs and tables, which are all still intact and neatly arranged. There's another heavy door to the kitchen, and inside the greenish phosphorescent ceiling strips provide enough light to see, just about. It's all very tidy. When the last people left, they weren't in too much of a hurry, and they were conscientious enough to clean up after themselves. They probably hoped they'd be coming back.

Disappointingly, the cupboards are empty other than pans and plates. I lift the lid of a chest fridge. There's not much inside, but my tummy growls at the sight of what there is. The veg is no good, and the milk smells like death. I root around for a while and pull out a box.

Bingo. The Excelsior never was a destination for fine dining. I'd always suspected most of the ingredients came pre-made.

I jab at the box, my gloved fingers fumbling with the packaging, then I pull out my drink pouch and yank the bottle out. There's plenty of water in my suit's main tank – this one's just for alternative liquid sources. Let's face it, that usually means alcohol.

There's a knack to this. I ease out one of the precooked Yorkshire puddings and pull off chunks, so that it starts to look like the eroded wave barrier outside. I crumble the chunks between my fingers and drop crumbs into the bottle. Once it's half-full, I connect up the bottle and close the flap.

Like I say, it's not fine dining. But sucking Yorkshire pudding crumbs through a straw sounds worse than it is.

The food calms my stomach, which in turn calms my mind. I leave the restaurant smiling and then saunter out of the hotel airlock.

And then I see a black shape either side of me and I turn toward one of them with my hands up, totally unprepared for the attack. At precisely the same moment that I realise that the black-visored, angular suit before me has all the hallmarks of a prospector's cobbled-together, scrawled-upon and sand-blasted aesthetic, the person who's now beyond my peripheral vision hits me with a piledriver smack to the head.

Twenty

I wake up with the mother of all hangovers.

I'm cold.

I open my eyes, or rather one of them, because the eyelids of the left one are glued together. Now I recognise the taste in my mouth too. Blood. Worse still, *my* blood.

Those fucking prospectors.

I shiver and blink my one good eye to clear my vision. My wrists sting like buggery and my arms are held behind me, the backs of my hands on the dusty floor.

Blearily, I make out that my legs appear black. Which means I'm wearing my jeans. Which means I'm not wearing my suit.

I take a tentative breath, as if I haven't been breathing all this time I've been knocked out. The air's fine. So there's that.

Everything's all swimmy as I look around. The room is dim. There's a churchlike silence, which makes me wonder if I'm back at the chapel, especially when I make out the rows of seats in front of me. But there are only four rows of seats, and they're comfy-looking with reddish synthetic upholstery, like cinema seats. They're positioned slightly below the platform on which I'm slumped like a discarded doll.

I twist my neck awkwardly to rub my left eye on the shoulder of my T-shirt. I squeak at the flash of pain, but after a bit more careful rubbing I can see again through my sticky eyelashes. There must be an open wound somewhere above the eyebrow, but I've had worse injuries even just in these last few months. Something's up with my lungs, though – my breathing keeps catching. My guess is that the prospector that attacked me punctured my suit visor. Wherever I am now can't be far from the Excelsior, otherwise I'd have asphyxiated. The image of

Jerem Ferrer floats before my eyes but I sure as hell don't appreciate the symmetry of our situations.

Where am I?

On the wall to my left are a series of placards filled with dense writing, too small to read in the dim light. To my right is a curtain, some synthetic material doing a pretty good job of looking like crushed velvet. Perhaps this really is a cinema.

With a bit of work, I manage to turn to look behind me, expecting a screen.

This'll amuse you: I make this ugly, high-pitched yelp when I see what I'm tied to. Nobody's brave all the time.

The aye-aye looks big, but that's only because I'm tied to its ankles. It's the pose that's unnerving: one arm stub on its chest, the other raised high above me. My first impression is that it's about to strike me on the head – *not again*, is what I'm thinking – until I realise that it's not moving, and that the pose is more like an opera singer delivering an aria than a merciless assailant.

And it's wearing a dress, so there's that too.

I shuffle and try to free my wrists.

"Lift your feet up?" I whisper. When the aye-aye doesn't respond, I say, "Wake. Power on."

Nothing.

Another twist of the head, another realisation. The aye-aye wouldn't be able to release me even if it could raise its heavy feet. There's a pole extending from the platform – the stage? – which pierces its smooth thigh. The aye-aye's a permanent fixture.

There are other poles behind me to either side, too. There are more aye-ayes fixed upon them, though they're in worse states than the one I'm bound to. One has a missing leg and no head. The other's barely more than a torso on a pole, a robot lollipop.

It's all really weird.

I shake my head to try and shift the dizziness but, as you might imagine, that doesn't work too well. So instead I turn my attention to my hands. They're bound with thick cord, maybe electrical cable. Contorting them, I can feel that the pole supporting the dress-wearing aye-aye isn't cylindrical. That is, it has sharp corners. Rub rub rub goes the cable against the pole, but you know what? My arms weren't designed to move like that, behind my back. My shoulders keep clicking. Feels as if my arms will fall off before long and I'll be left like that lollipop-torso aye-aye.

Still. What else am I going to do? So after a breather I start again, bunching up my legs to gain more purchase on the surface of the stage, pushing my weight forwards to add pressure to the cable. Before long I'm doing awkward bunny-hops, my knees and shoulders shouting with pain, my head going peek-a-boo in and out of the folds of the aye-aye's yellow summer dress.

I realise I'm making a total racket. I blame the concussion, the oxygen depletion.

I stop and listen. Still not a sound from outside the room.

Okay, good. Start again.

But as soon as I start, my legs give way. I'm sprawled again on the stage, panting and swearing, so giddy that for a second I feel a wash of shame that I'm lying staring upwards beneath someone's dress.

Don't laugh. It's not funny.

I fill my aching lungs and scrabble to right myself, flailing my legs like a beetle on its back.

One of my feet hits something hard at the edge of the stage and then somebody starts singing.

My body starts jolting up and down. What's happening?

The aye-aye's moving. Its arms are waving to one side and then the other, graceful movements, so fluid that I can imagine its missing hands, invisible fingers dancing.

The melody's sweet, the voice angelic. The aye-aye dances in sync with the light fingerpicking of a ukelele. I turn to see the naked, headless aye-ayes bobbing smoothly up and down too. The effect is an entirely different breed of eerie to the convincing motion of the aye-aye above me.

Welcome to Hawaii, reads green lettering projected onto the wall directly behind me. Above that is a permanent sign, painted rather than projected: *Traditional Dances of Earth*.

It takes me a few seconds to realise what I've achieved. It's not just my aye-aye that's moving: the pole is sliding up and down, too.

I set to work again, pulling the cable tight against the sharp-cornered pole. It takes only a few minutes for the friction to wear away at the plastic covering of one side of the cable. A painful twist of the wrists and then the remaining part snaps.

"Ha!" I shout out, rubbing at my wrists and then my shoulders, glaring up at the dancing aye-aye as if it should acknowledge my breakthrough.

I roll off the stage, clamber onto one of the front row of seats. Get my breath back, maybe pass out for a few minutes.

The captive aye-ayes keep dancing. When I open my eyes again the music's harsher and more raucous. Honky-tonk piano and quacking trumpets; some tune from the 1920s that makes me picture flappers and speakeasies. The legs of the central aye-aye swing wildly, its feet crisscrossing as its arms windmill. All of a sudden, I feel ashamed for the aye-aye, its helplessness and lack of modesty. I reach up onto the stage, feel around for the hidden switch, flick it. The aye-aye freezes with its arms above its head, making me no less nauseous.

I've got to get out of here.

Beyond the curtains, the interior of the building is in even worse repair. There are more platforms and cabinets, a few poles with robot torsos attached, but most of the exhibits are completely destroyed. It can't be that the aye-ayes were stripped for parts, because the remnants of the exhibits litter the floor. I have to step over limbs and cracked aye-aye skulls to make my way through the building.

Room after room, all the same. The signs behind each platform are the only clues to the original dioramas. *The Plays of William Shakespeare. Manual Labour. Traditional Family Roles.* It all seems misguided, this idea that Earth tourists might appreciate seeing warped depictions of their own home lives, with details almost certainly lost in translation. One platform has more than a dozen poles, all unoccupied, with huge lettering that takes up the entire wall behind it: *Warfare*.

I reach a little foyer. To one side of a low counter are racks that maybe once held toys and novelties for sale. Behind the counter someone's daubed a message on the wall. The paint dripped so much before drying that it's almost illegible, so it takes me a few seconds to decipher it.

A.I.: AN INSULT

Each letter A and I are in red paint, the rest in black.

Interesting.

But it's beside the point. I need to find out where I am. I scoot to the front of the foyer, keeping close to one wall to avoid being seen from outside. To either side of the airlock are floor-to-ceiling windows, the only source of light in this part of the museum.

Most of the view is blocked by the sand-sculpted wave at the edge of the seafront. So I was right – I wasn't carried or dragged far after being attacked. There's nobody out there that I can see. I press myself flat against the window – its surface feels ice cold against my bare arms – and when I push my cheek against it with my head to one side, I can make out the piazza, the Excelsior... and the snub nose of the trawler I drove here.

So all I need to do is get to it.

But I don't have my suit.

I hurry through all of the rooms again, then check behind the foyer counter and in the few back rooms. There's no sign of my suit. That makes a kind of sense – the prospectors must have figured they could hack my wrist panel to gain access to my ship. I should be grateful that they decided not to slice off my head after all. It's a rookie mistake, really, and the fact that they left me here alive goes even further to suggest that they were a cowardly pair of chancers.

But the trouble is, there's no *other* suit either.

And, while the remains of the exhibition aye-ayes have been left scattered all over the place, the building's been totally gutted in every other sense. Most importantly, all the comms units have been stripped out by looters.

I don't have any way of contacting the outside world.

I can't begin to tell you how frustrating I find this whole situation. I'm fine. I'm fucking fine. But I'm trapped in a decaying museum in my abandoned childhood hometown, a mere fifty metres from my car and escape, and I didn't even think to tell anyone I was coming here.

Rookie mistake. Again.

Twenty-one

You know me. I'm never despondent for long.

For a few minutes I let myself imagine that Franck will figure out where I might have gone, that he'll swoop in and pull up a trundler outside the door. But he's new to the sidekick game. It could take him days or weeks to make any progress finding me, if ever.

And I can't help feeling that there's some urgency to this investigation, now.

And yeah, I'm partly thinking of you, too.

But soon enough I pull myself together. I find a mirror, clean up the blood from the slash on my forehead, use the curtains to wipe away the sweat from my armpits.

Then I head to the workshop I spotted earlier. Find a hammer and a wrench, return to the museum exhibits, set to work.

Before long I'm surrounded by aye-aye parts, mostly torsos. They're not the easiest things to work with, but where there's a will there's a way.

I'm not heartless by nature. I don't enjoy doing what I'm doing. I apologise to each of them as I crack their bodies in two.

You'd have done the same thing in my position. If that were possible.

The workshop is well-stocked – whoever ransacked the museum were not only Luddites, they were imbeciles. There's plenty of acetylene for the welding torch. Some of these tools are worth a mint and, more importantly, they're *good*. They're mostly steel, which means they were imported from Earth, which means they've lasted more than twenty years since the final ships arrived.

But just because I have the tools doesn't mean I can work miracles.

I know, I know. A bad workman…

Anyway, it doesn't have to be perfect. It just has to get me the hell out of here, and even then only as far as the trundler.

When I'm finished I stand back to admire my handiwork. It'd have been an easier build if I wasn't such a big girl. I've had to make the thing a head taller than I am to allow for the double-thickness of its walls, and a bit of wiggle room. It has the dimensions of a generously-sized sofa standing on one end. All that curved plastic looks decidedly grubbier than when I found it, marked with welding burns and ugly ripples where I've forced the pieces of the aye-ayes into new shapes.

The fact that it's difficult as hell to drag the thing to the front of the foyer doesn't inspire confidence. But if I'm honest I'm less worried about the weight – I tend to be able to summon reserves of energy when I'm in a fix – and more about whether or not the suit's airtight. I can't test it, you see, without smashing a window and letting all the air get sucked out of the building. So I figure I might as well test it out on the road. If I'm not killed instantly, I can scurry back into the airlock. Right?

There's nothing for it. I take a long look at the airlock controls, then out of the window, trying to commit it all to memory. Then I duck down, crawl under the suit, and then ease myself up inside. Once I'm there, I wiggle to find a standing position that doesn't result in the pivots at each joint jabbing into my flesh.

Then I pull the hinged bottom section up, using the cables tied to the hatches. It barely even clicks as it closes.

The most awkward part next: I contort my body to reach down with the blowtorch. I spit and curse as I weld shut the hatch as best I can.

It's not my most graceful moment, I can tell you.

When I'm done I give myself exactly one minute to rest.

I take a deep breath.

I've only given the suit a single arm – the right one – to cut down on the amount of exposed joints. And of course, far more annoyingly, I wasn't able to give myself a visor. Where the head should be is just a continuation of the bulky, hollow box.

The plastic resists my efforts as I reach my arm up and prod blindly at where the airlock controls should be. I don't get any tactile feedback but I hear a distant click and then the huff of the door opening.

I operate each leg in turn, gritting my teeth at the difficulty of even the simplest action. The welding might keep me alive, but it's made the joints stiff as hell.

I'm *pretty* sure I'm inside the airlock now.

I reach up, slow as a glacier. It takes me more than a minute to locate the button.

Huff, goes the airlock door, then *huff* again as the air's sucked out.

I grit my teeth.

I count to five, then step forward.

Even trapped in this coffin, I sense the quality of light changing. I'm outside.

And I'm still alive.

I'm not actually breathing, though. I'll save that for when there's no alternative. I've timed myself in the past. I can hold my breath for two minutes, easy. But my lungs are already knackered from my last experience of being partially exposed to the vacuum of Mars, and you know what? At this moment I'm not in peak condition.

But I always give this sort of thing my best shot. It's kind of my trademark.

I try not to let myself grunt as I push against first one leg and then the other, but it's hard not to, and every so often I snort, expelling what little air's in me, clogging my suit with carbon dioxide.

The suit feels heavy as lead, and the joints barely bend so I'm hobbling forwards little by little. I reckon I've moved ten metres from the museum. Maybe.

Step, step, step. Brief pause. Step, step. Okay, another break.

This isn't going to be enough. I'm not even certain I'm heading in the right direction. Which is bad – but on the other hand, it also means I'm far from sure of being able to find my way back to the airlock, which actually works as an odd sort of motivation. Might as well press on.

Step, step.

There's a funny hissing sound.

No point in looking down. Hurry up instead.

I shift all my weight forward, trying to concentrate on the agonisingly slow rhythm, building up to another step while the other leg is still in the process of thudding down.

I swear I'm getting faster, but that hissing sound is getting louder too. And there's this pressure against my skin, a sucking sensation rather than pushing. Soon I'll be out of air.

Step, step, step, step, leaning forward more and more, gaining momentum, tilting like a charging knight in armour but a whole lot less dramatic.

I hear a little click. It's hardly anything at all.

But the pain.

I can't stop myself from looking down. The weld's starting to give way on the hatch. Through the hairline crack I can see the Martian surface scudding beneath me.

Fuckity fuck.

I close my eyes – I can't see anything anyway – and that helps for a few more moments, making the pain dreamlike and weirdly remote. But the suction builds up more and more, mingling with the hangover headache I already had, and my jaw aches as though all my teeth are being slowly extracted at once. And still my legs are moving, as though it's not me controlling them, as if it's just the product of the momentum I've built up. I can feel the weals and bruises forming on my thighs with each slow step I take.

There's a series of little snipping sounds. More pressure. A fogginess somewhere inside me, growing.

At times like this I like to develop a little mantra to keep my mind on track.

Oh shit oh shit oh shit oh shit oh shit.

Step, step, step, step, step, no time for stopping, step, step.

I'm leaning forward further and further. I'm a diagonal person in a diagonal coffin. I can't remember exactly what I'm doing here.

I'm falling.

I can't breathe.

I really am falling.

I'm so giddy that it's almost funny, the idea of me toppling forward, the knowledge that from the outside I must appear as inert as a brick even though in here I'm flailing and floundering.

So funny!

I must stop laughing. The only thing I can do is to force my one arm up as if it might stop me from falling onto the Martian surface and never getting up.

It does.

It does stop me.

I'm still tilting forward to a dangerous degree, but I'm still upright, more or less.

I try to move my arm. Can't.

The pressure in my head keeps telling me all this is funny.

It fucking isn't.

Another attempt, and this time the arm of the suit moves and then lurches.

I'm leaning on something.

Maybe?

Maybe the trundler?

That would be nice.

Two new problems. One: stop leaning forward like a mime artist in the wind. Two: get the hell into the trundler. Do you know what? I'm not sure I actually thought this far ahead into my plan.

I push backward, then scrabble my way into the upper part of the suit, my knees against my chest. I rock forward and backwards, forwards and backwards. Finally, I feel the suit lifting from its resting position. I throw myself down into my starting position just in time for the suit to come to a halt wobbling on its lumpy feet.

I'm puffed out, literally. There's no air left. I can feel my eyeballs bulging beneath my eyelids and a vice around every limb. I'm so sore, so unhappy.

I'm sobbing as I manage to raise the arm of the suit again. With the suit's arm and my arm inside it outstretched, I prod at the air, shift it a little, prod, shift, prod. I see faces against the pulsing orange of my eyelids: Franck, Hazel, along with hazy silhouettes that I suppose are my parents. Nobody from Earth.

I feel a jolt as something impacts against the top of the suit, where the helmet would normally be.

I pray that I know what I've hit. The door of the trundler swinging open. Please let it be.

Now I'm pushing forward again, literally breathless, with no plan B. If I fall face first into the dust then that's the end of me.

The suit bumps against something, pivots heavily around the middle, teeters forward and then thumps flat. My face smacks against the hard interior.

"Close door!" I scream.

The most beautiful sound, the most beautiful sensation. A hushed whisper, a lungful of air.

I'm in the trundler. I'm kind of incredible.

I'm very sleepy.

But I want out of this coffin. After a break of only a handful of seconds I scrunch my legs and then kick at the hatch. It comes away at the first impact. Who knows how many more seconds it would have lasted, out there.

The sharp edges of the suit lacerate the skin of my arms and neck as I struggle free. Who the hell cares.

I climb up onto the enormous suit, this Frankenstein's monster made of robotic corpses, that fills most of the front seat of the trundler.

I let my head fall back. Summoning up all the air that's now filling my lungs once again, I howl in triumph at the roof, at the sky.

I feel all sorts of awesome.

Until I look out through the windscreen.

There, on the bonnet of the trundler, spreadeagled like a sacrifice, is my own white suit.

Twenty-two

Franck's waiting for me in the cargo bay. I can tell from his crumpled expression that he's been fretting. I steer the trundler as best I can through the airlock bay, but the doors seem narrower than I remember and my hands keep slipping on the wheel. I'm pretty close to passing out.

Franck pauses for a second when he spots my white suit on the bonnet of the vehicle. It didn't make the journey back from the coast any easier, I can tell you, keeping the suit balanced there despite all the bumps of the Martian surface and the barely-sculpted tracks. A couple of times I had to scold myself because my mind strayed to thoughts of putting on my aye-aye suit again, just for a few minutes, to nip out and fetch my own suit. Each time I looked down at the mass of scorched plastic in the footwell – it's so big that I've had to drive with my feet up on the seat, like a trained ape – and each time I told myself: *Don't be a dick.*

I'm leaning on the door of the trundler when Franck opens it. I half-fall and Franck isn't big enough to catch me, but he eases me to the floor with a grunt.

"What happened?" he asks.

"Mislaid my suit."

He looks up at the bonnet. "How did it get –"

Then, over my shoulder, he notices the desecration of a dozen aye-ayes that fills most of the cabin.

I shake my head. "Don't let three-eight-three see that. Okay?"

I shouldn't move my head like that. Very dizzy. I put my hand up to my forehead and it comes away bloody.

"Somebody attacked you," Franck says. Then, "Why are you grinning?"

"Because this shows we're onto something."

"Shall I call a medic?"

"Nah. I've had worse."

"But who did this to you?"

I shrug, then wince. "Two of them. They looked like prospectors."

He helps me up to a sitting position, leaning against the caterpillar tracks of the trundler. "Those psychos from Pearl Bay? Munch and Clem?"

"No. And I only said they *looked* like prospectors."

"Meaning what? That they weren't really?"

"Even if prospectors wanted to derail this investigation, I'm certain they'd *also* want to find a way off-world. But they didn't take my head, and they didn't take my suit. Didn't even have the guts to kill me."

Franck gives me a funny look. I'm not saying I *wanted* to be killed. I just don't appreciate people not doing their jobs properly.

"So…"

I sigh. "I'm not very comfy here. Help me up?"

In truth, Franck doesn't do much to support me as I lurch to my feet, but just the fact of him trying is enough. We stumble over to a bench against one wall of the cargo bay. Franck sweeps the accumulated tools and magazines onto the floor. We slump onto the bench side by side, then I teeter towards Franck. He stands again, lets me fall slowly to horizontal. He paces up and down while I lie on my back with my eyes closed.

"You were about to explain," Franck says.

"Was I?" I murmur. "I don't think I was. You tell me the answer and then I'll explain it to you."

"Abbey."

I don't open my eyes. I lift my heavy hands, as if I might pluck facts and conclusions from the darkness. "Some people – two people, at least – think that we're getting close to the truth. Or maybe another outcome they don't want. They're panicking. And they're unprofessional."

"Because they didn't kill you?"

I gesture vaguely at the trundler. "Because they didn't follow through in any sense. If they wanted to look like prospectors, they should have taken my suit, then my ship. My guess is they didn't know what to do with either of them. Maybe they had an idea of my death looking like suicide, but even then it's absurd. They locked me in an abandoned building with no suit and no comms, just playing for time."

"To achieve what?"

"That's the trouble. It's one thing to deduce the intentions of professionals. Systematic actions, clear, logical. But amateurs... *so* annoying."

Franck keeps pacing, regular as a metronome.

"Are you thinking?" I say. My words are getting a bit slurred. I need to sleep. "Or just exercising?"

"This means..." Franck says, sounding more far away all the time, though that could just be because of my concussion and oxygen starvation. "It means that these people don't want you to conclude that aye-aye three-eight-three is a murderer. Because that's what we think, isn't it? That's what the video feed showed?"

I don't answer. Time passes.

"Abbey? Are you asleep?"

"Don't know about that," I say.

"You don't know if you're asleep?"

They don't know about that.

I heave myself upright. I'm kind of surprised to find myself still on the bench in the cargo bay, rather than in a bed, or in the midst of the storm that was starting to creep in from the edges of my vision.

"They don't know about that," I say. "Don't you see? Whoever attacked me, it's perfectly possible that they don't know about the evidence we've uncovered that supports three-eight-three's guilt. Which means that something else I've been doing has made me a threat."

"Okay. Okay. Like what?"

I shake my head again. It's the wrong question.

"Abbey? What are you thinking? I can't read your mind."

I stare up at him, his too-small facial features, his frizzy hair. "That's what I'm *talking* about, Franck. You can't read my mind, and neither can they."

I stand, falter a bit, have a word with myself, straighten up my huge aching body.

"Whatever this is," I say, "it's all about communication."

Twenty-three

"Wind it back," I say to Franck. "Once again, from the top."

Franck sighs but restarts the footage.

I put my arm around Ai383's smooth shoulders. "Please. Watch closely. Try to remember."

I've rigged up a projector, and the enlarged video on the workshop wall makes it even more pixelated than before. It's easy enough to identify *what* we're seeing, but figuring out the emotional content of Ferrer's expression is much harder, and even a professional lipreader would struggle to understand what he's saying.

"Do you recall the nature of your experiments on the native Martians?" I say softly.

"No," Ai383 replies.

"Do you remember Jerem Ferrer?"

"I remember him in death. I remember him from this video footage."

I point at the image of Ferrer's huge, moving lips. "If you had to guess, what do you think he's saying right now?"

"He is gesticulating at his helmet and he is forming words that are unintelligible. I cannot guess."

"Then I'll tell you what *I* would guess. I'd say he's commanding you to remove his helmet."

"And yet I could not perform such a task. He would be unable to breathe."

"Yeah." I rub at my eyes. My legs ache and my clothes stink.

The video reaches its end. Ferrer's bulging eyes, his terror. Then black.

"What do you think is happening to Jerem Ferrer right now, in this footage?"

Ai383 seems uncertain. Then, "He appears to be in the early stages of asphyxiation."

I nod slowly. "Pause it, Franck?"

Gently, I turn Ai383's body until she's facing me. "Look. I'm trying to help you here, okay? What you're saying is an admission of guilt. It doesn't matter that what you did *should* be impossible. If you did it, you did it. And there will be repercussions." I don't elaborate. *For you, and for all of your kind.*

Even before the aye-aye responds, I can sense this is a dead end.

"I cannot guess," Ai383 says again.

Twenty-four

When Hazel answers the door, surprise is written all over her face.

"I honestly never thought I'd hear from you again," she says.

I give her a sheepish grin. "Yeah. Well, I wondered if I could use your bath."

She steps aside to let me into her quarters. She's wearing shorts and an old pullover that's far too big for her. Maybe it belonged to her uncle, in which case it might even be real wool rather than synthetic.

"Long day?" she says and even though her nose hardly wrinkles, I know she must be appalled at the smell that's coming off me. At least Franck made sure to tidy up my forehead wound before he reluctantly let me leave the workshop.

I don't reply, and once I'm inside I hover uncertainly in the centre of the room. Hazel comes on over and kisses me on my cheek and I swear I could fall in love with her just for overcoming the stink.

"Bathroom's that way," she says, then laughs. "Sorry. You already know that."

She leaves me alone as I strip, trying to ignore the purple bruises blooming on my thighs. I fill the bath and slip in, bending my knees to fit in as much of my lanky body as possible. It's scalding hot and I like it. I rummage through the bottles lined up on the side. I bet these weren't around when Jerem lived here: they're scented with lime, camomile, mango. I squeeze a few into the water and bubbles start to form right away, hiding the floating pools of scum I've already put on the surface.

I lie staring at the ceiling and not thinking about my parents. Instead, I play with the bubbles, lifting up clods of them, blowing them so they float up and then back down to land on my nose.

Now I'm trying not to think of the storm dream, too. I groan, then lift my buttocks so that I slide down towards the taps and my head goes under the surface.

I have a good old shout, safe now that the only things that come out of my mouth are bubbles of air.

When I come up again, Hazel's standing in the doorway.

"I'd ask if there was room for a little one," she says. Her eyes travel down my body, to my legs – one bent awkwardly underwater, the other knee poking high above the surface. Her eyelids flicker when she notices my bruises, but they she finds her composure. "But, you know."

So instead she kneels on the bathmat, her elbows plonked on the edge of the tub.

We don't speak, only look at each other, a bit of a smile. It feels like enough for now.

But eventually she says, "Anything you want to talk about?"

I grimace. "You sound just like someone I spoke to today."

"Oh?"

"Yeah. You mentioned him the last time we..." I feel my cheeks flush. "...met. Reverend Guillaume."

"That old crackpot? Please don't tell me you went there on personal business, Abbey."

I think of Guillaume's desk terminal, the logs of colonists. Meryl and Richard. "No. It was about the case."

Hazel's expression darkens. "I'm not sure we ought to discuss the case. I have a lot at stake, don't forget. I wouldn't want to compromise any evidence or influence you."

I shake my head. "But I want to talk about it. I need to." I don't hide the note of pleading. I'm okay being naked in front of Hazel, in every way.

"All right."

"Just like that, you change your mind?"

"I trust you. So. All right."

I shuffle to raise myself up in the bath. "He's got me rattled, that's all. And if I'm honest, I'm struggling to work out what's related to your uncle's case and what isn't."

Hazel studies my face. Then her eyes dart. "Let me guess. He started banging on about a universal language. Yes?"

"Yes. How did you –"

"Because it's his pet topic. My uncle's too. Except Jerem didn't make suppositions – to put it in scientific terms, he didn't proceed from axioms. He was just interested."

"And what about Guillaume?"

"It's all ideological with somebody like that. Any shred of evidence is filtered through layers and layers of theology, prejudice, bigotry."

I try to attach each of those words to Guillaume in my mind. It's hard to tell if they stick.

Hazel sighs. "Maybe you're not as perceptive as you seem. Don't take that the wrong way. I've no doubt you're excellent at your work. And anyway, it's obvious that you've picked up on the Reverend's essential shadiness. This talk about communication. It's only ever zealotry."

I think of the congregation. I got the sense that they'd lap up any explanation, anything to feel less alone. "There are other colonists who feel like that?"

She shrugs. "Probably. But that's not what I mean. Guillaume's the most recent in a long line of fanatics, though of course it's a new breed here on Mars. You have to know your history. Some of these historical projects were perfectly benign, even admirable. Take Esperanto, though it was doomed because there was no essential *need* for people to learn a whole extra language. But the bad ones were always obsessed on religious grounds."

"Guillaume mentioned Babel. Which was a tower, right?"

Hazel rolls her eyes. "Go further back. Here's the nub of it: when God said 'Fiat lux', what language did he speak?"

"It's Latin. Let there be light."

She reaches out, passes her hand in front of my eyes. "There's no light in there, that's for sure. 'Fiat lux' is only an approximation. Nobody could speak in the language God used, not any more, because of the whole Babel incident. Which I can explain to you, I guess?"

I wave a hand airily. I'm not going out of my way to highlight my ignorance.

"Long story short," she says. "A bunch of people get ideas above their station. Quite literally. They work together – working bloody hard, mind you – on a tower with the intention of making it so high it reaches heaven. Wouldn't it be fun to poke around up there? And God's righteously pissed off and, creative as ever, he decides the best punishment is first to scatter everyone around the world, and then to 'confound their language' – thereby simultaneously preventing another project of such overreaching ambition, and simultaneously kickstarting the tourism and translation industries."

"But what about that language, the first one…"

"The original language, yes. Some call it the perfect language. Perfect, because not only was it the language of God, it also revealed the true nature of things. So, whatever the word for dog might be, the word itself would convey the *essence* of dogness: four legs, loyal, stupid, floppy tongue, that funny smell they have… everything. And for some reason, people like Guillaume think that speaking in that language would be ace. Me, I think it would be stiflingly literal, but there you go. Jerem always disagreed with me too, but at least I could argue with him in good humour."

"Did you ever talk to Guillaume about it?"

"Nope. I heard a few of his sermons, and Jerem gave me potted summaries of their endless discussions. I left well alone. I can only imagine how he'd argue the case for James the Fourth of Scotland, who sent two young children to be reared in silence by some random mute woman on a remote island. Or Frederick the Second, the Holy Roman Emperor. Ever hear of him? He ran language deprivation experiments – using children again, of course, always children, for pity's sake. So these groups of newborns were kept in isolation, not allowed to hear any words in any language. The hope in each case was that when the doors were flung open a handful of years later, these kids would have spontaneously learned to speak in a tongue untainted by the babble of modern languages, and old James and Frederick and all the rest of those vicious bastards would lay bets on whether that natural language might be Greek, or Latin, or Hebrew, or something entirely new."

I watch the play of emotions on Hazel's face. It must be nice to feel so passionate about something so abstract. It must feel good to be able to convey your opinions so strongly. There's nothing holding her back. Babel or no Babel, she has total clarity.

It's a nice face, too. I'm not so good at reading people from their expressions, but Hazel's different. It's another form of communication, maybe more revealing than words.

Hold on.

I've burst out of the bath before I've even told my body to move. Hazel's on her haunches and she topples backwards in shock. I leap out onto the bathmat, brush aside the towel that Hazel holds out to me, and start pulling clothes onto my dripping body.

Twenty-five

"What's his suit got to do with it?" Hazel says, hurrying to keep up with me as I stride towards the lab. "I don't understand what you're mumbling about."

"Nearly there," I say, increasing my pace.

The helmets are piled up alongside the racks of suits. I rifle through them, muttering. These are the suits Franck and I wore, but where's –

I recognise Ferrer's helmet from the video footage, because there's a smiley-face sticker stuck to the bottom-right under the visor. I struggle into one of the suits, then pull on Ferrer's helmet. I try not to imagine his disapproval.

I throw another of the suits to Hazel. "You don't have to come in. Just talk to me on the radio, okay?"

Watching me, Hazel gets into the suit. It's too big for her but it hardly matters. When she's got it on I take one of the spare helmets at random, then twist it into place. I gesture toward the back of my hand, where the comms controls are. Hazel taps her button.

"– going to explain yourself any time soon?" she says over the comms link, loud and clear.

My heart sinks. Bang goes that theory.

"I'm sorry," I reply. "I thought I had a lead."

Hazel makes a face. She points at my wrist control.

I hold it up to show her that I've already activated comms. "Hey. Are you telling me you can't hear me?"

Hazel squints at me, then her voice comes through clearly, "What are you saying to me? I can't hear a word."

And *there* it is.

I take her hand and drag her into the airlock centre of the Venn diagram. I glance at the sofa. For the first time it occurs to me that the blanket that Hazel mentioned, the one that Ferrer slept under when he would spend the night here in his lab, is nowhere to be seen.

I tap at the single terminal, hardly slowed down by the bulky gloves, rooting through the files and folders held on Caraway's cloud drive.

I set the captured video footage playing. The familiar image of the Martian crab skittering around within its transparent barriers, Ai383's blue arm stubs appearing in view every couple of seconds.

"Abbey, what is this?" Hazel says, turning to stare at me even though her suit is still facing the screen.

I hold up a hand, then make a circling-finger gesture. *Let it run.*

It's only when Ferrer's wrinkled face appears that it occurs to me just how inappropriate it is to have Hazel watch this footage. My ears are burning, but I swallow my remorse. I'm on a roll and I brake for nobody.

I almost push Hazel out of the way to get closer to the little screen. Ferrer points with both hands at his helmet – this helmet, the one I'm wearing now. He mouths words and even though this terminal doesn't have audio output, I imagine the dull pops and clicks which show that audio was being recorded, except not his speech. I watch his lips. He could be saying a whole lot of different things, but it's not inconceivable he's saying *Are you trying to tell me you can't hear me?* or something to that effect.

And then Ai383's arms reach up either side of the helmet – this helmet – and then they twist and lift.

I feel awful for Hazel. She's not making a peep, but I'm a fucking monster, making her watch this.

Ferrer's eyes go wide and I don't need a lipreader to tell me that he's making instinctive feral sounds of terror, not words.

And then black.

I should get Hazel out of here. I shouldn't do what I'm about to do.

I hit the button on the wall that begins the depressurisation process.

"Abbey," Hazel says. Just that.

I mouth the words, "Trust me," but I know she doesn't, not now. But that's good.

There's a red light and a beep to signal that depressurisation is complete. I point at the oxygen readout, waiting a second for Hazel to understand what it means.

I reach out both my hands towards Hazel.

She backs away but bumps into the terminal. She shakes her head. "Abbey. What? What the hell are you doing?"

I shush her, but I know she can only see the shape of my mouth. I reach up, fast, and put one hand on either side of her helmet.

I make a quick twisting motion. Hazel doesn't know it, but I've loosened my grip so that my fingers are only grazing the surface of the helmet – I don't have enough purchase to actually remove it.

But there. I see it, right in front of me.

I had to see it for myself.

That expression, precisely the same as Jerem Ferrer's. Not asphyxiation at all – just profound shock, panic rising suddenly from nowhere, and the conviction that death is only seconds away.

Twenty-six

Franck finds me sitting cross-legged on the floor of the cargo bay. I'm wearing my comfortable old suit now instead of Ferrer's. I spent a while patching up the pinprick hole in the visor, and now I'm playing Alice Coltrane through my helmet speakers but even she can't help.

"What's happened?" he says when he sees my face.

Instinctively, I raise my hand to rub at my eyes, but just end up tapping uselessly at my visor. "I think I fucked up."

"The case?"

I frown. "What? No."

"Oh." He doesn't seem to know what to say. Maybe he feels I'm being unprofessional, if this is a personal matter. But we're all human, aren't we?

"Do you want to talk about it?" he says slowly.

I groan. "Why does everyone keep asking me that? No, Franck, I don't want to talk about it. I want to get very far away from here. Want to come?"

He glances at the door. "Pannick's demanding results. She's threatening to call Sagacity direct."

"She won't. But I get what you're saying. My welcome's wearing thin. But you didn't answer my question."

Franck clucks his tongue. "Hell yes."

He pulls on a suit and helmet while I settle into the driver's seat of our AkTrak. He hops in. As the cargo door opens, he says, "Where are we going?"

"Out."

He goes quiet. I might as well have brought an aye-aye driver, because I'm taking it slow and steady.

After a few minutes I say, "I think better when I'm driving."

But in actual fact I can't remember anything I *have* been thinking about, other than Hazel's expression when I pretended to pull off her helmet, and then her expression after she'd stumbled out of the airlock, shed her suit and glared at me before legging it out of the lab.

Over the comms I hear Franck wetting his lips. "What are you thinking about?" he says.

I force Hazel out of my mind. "The video footage doesn't show Ferrer asking for his helmet to be removed. His voice comms unit was faulty. He couldn't speak to aye-aye three-eight-three."

I turn. Franck's still staring out at the red track ahead of us, blinking rapidly. "So when he pointed at his helmet…"

"He was complaining to three-eight-three. Yeah."

"But even if that's the case, the aye-aye knew that removing the helmet would mean murdering him."

Hazel's face swims into view again. "He didn't asphyxiate."

Franck's posture loosens. He taps the dashboard a couple of times. "Abbey. He *did* asphyxiate. I examined his corpse myself."

"Yeah. So I need time to think. Tell me more about Ferrer."

Franck takes a deep breath. "You know all the salient details. He was motivated, intellectual. A loner, by choice. Most of his regular contacts were off-base, other than his niece." He pauses, and I don't want to check to see if he's looking at me. "While Pannick had to update his permissions periodically, his funding was provided in totality by Sandcastle management, and everyone in the chain seemed happy enough to turn a blind eye to his procurement of native Martians from the diamond prospectors."

I nod. All old news.

"And when did he start his research?" I say. I have that hollow feeling in my stomach that I always get when I'm clutching at straws.

"When Caraway ground to a halt. Before that point Ferrer was gainfully employed. He worked within the logistics team, sifting through data to pinpoint suitable sites for colonies, even for cities to be established, though that seems an utter joke in retrospect. We were still theoretically hunting for city sites five years after Earth had already made the decision that there wouldn't *be* any new cities."

The trundler emerges from the steep-sided sculpted track and then we're on the open plain. The bumping softens as the caterpillar tracks sink into the top layer of dust. I consider heading to the coast, but the thought of that kind of indulgence makes me queasy, especially with Franck in tow. So where to?

Then a thought hits me.

"Franck!"

He jerks in his seat at the volume of my voice through his earpiece.

"Franck – you said Ferrer started his research when Caraway stopped crawling. But which stop are you talking about – the first or the second?"

His forehead goes all wrinkly. "The first time. That is, when the commands from base stopped. Those of us who wanted to keep active petitioned Pannick for approval for projects. They were mostly related to maintenance, or staff motivation. Ferrer's project was a bit more highbrow."

I thump the steering wheel happily. "And do you remember the coordinates of that first location?"

"Yeah, of course. Every time I left the base in a trundler from that site I'd have had to punch it in."

"Do it, Franck. Punch it in."

He fiddles with the dashboard screen and a directional arrow flashes up. I wrench the steering wheel right until we're facing the thin strip of sunrise. It feels good to have a sense of purpose.

It takes us maybe forty minutes, with me gunning the engine, until the screen flashes red. Franck's polite enough not to draw attention to the lurching of the trundler, but he's been holding onto a harness dangling from the roof the whole time.

"Show me," I say.

Franck bends forward, squinting into the sunlight. "There won't be much to see. But... there, due west a bit. There it is."

I'm out of the door before the AkTrak comes to a complete stop. My bruised thighs flash with pain as I land on the Martian surface. Franck parks up and follows slowly, obviously bemused.

All that's left of Caraway's previous site are two long linear heaps, hundreds of metres in length, which are more defined at one end than the other. That must be where the sand had piled up against Caraway's sides over the nine months it was stationed here, hardening in the centre over time and then disturbed only a little as it crawled away.

I stride along the outside of the nearest tall dust pile. Nothing, nothing, nothing, other than a few discarded food packets embedded in the sand.

"What are you looking for?" Franck calls out, making me jump. He should know he doesn't need to shout when we have working comms.

"One sec," I say.

I make my way around the end of the first heap and cross the wide area to reach the other strip. I'm holding my breath as I round the end of it. Now I can see all the way along to where Franck's standing with his hands on his hips.

Shit. I can't see anything out of the ordinary.

I take my time, scuffing my boots through the dust as I walk.

Two-thirds of the way along, my right foot hits something.

I scrabble in the dust to reveal a curved section of wall. It's about a foot tall – ground level must have risen slightly as a barchan dune sailed over this location, depositing part of its load as it went – and it's smooth and rounded at the top.

By the time Franck reaches me I'm already knee-deep in sand. Caramel-coloured dust rains down on me as I dislodge lower parts of the pile. I bet the stains will never come out of my suit.

Franck pitches in even though it's clear he thinks I've lost the plot. Before long we've pushed enough sand aside to reveal a curved wall.

But it's a ruin. At its highest point it's only maybe four feet.

"This is Ferrer's first lab," Franck says, finally cottoning on.

"Yeah."

"And that's exciting why, exactly?"

My hands flop against my sides. "It seemed like something, when it occurred to me."

"So. What next?"

I groan. "How about brunch?"

Franck manages a supportive chuckle. Then he starts chattering about the catering options at Tharsis Caraway, his hospitality training kicking in. But I'm not listening. I bend forwards with my hands on my knees, looking at the inside of the curved wall we've revealed, where I can make out the bottom part of a long, diagonal fissure.

Twenty-seven

We're silent all the way back to Tharsis Caraway, and Franck's sensible enough to leave me to my thoughts. Communication's all well and good, but sometimes *not* communicating is just as important.

Once we're parked up in the cargo bay, I say, "Right. I need access to the logs of sculptor activity."

Franck nods and scurries away. I follow him to the workshop. While he's tapping away at the terminal I glance over at Ai383 hanging in her locker. *I'm doing this for you*, I think, but who knows if that's true?

"Okay," Franck says, and stands aside to let me sit at the terminal.

It's all dated chronologically, with each new set of commands representing a new set of instructions given to the sculptor robots.

"What month did Caraway leave its previous site, almost five years ago?" I ask.

Franck squints. "June? July. One of the two."

I nod, then get back to flicking through the records. If the base shifted in June or July, then Ferrer's first lab must have been constructed at some point during the nine months before that. There aren't all that many records of sculptor activity, because for most of that time Pannick would have clung onto the hope that Caraway was just about to receive new commands. There wouldn't have been much call for permanent structures. Most of the instruction packages relate to roads and the odd outpost to act as a halfway house or supply store for investigations of the local area. Each construction job has an image attachment showing the relevant schematic.

As soon as I find it, it's obvious. In January of the same year, three sculptors were instructed to build a permanent structure on the east side of Tharsis Caraway, almost touching the caterpillar treads and connected by reinforced corridor. That's the lab we uncovered an hour ago, the ruined one. I click on the attachment to bring up a blueprint showing the Venn diagram layout of the lab, airlocks and all.

"What are you trying to prove?" Franck says, hovering over my shoulder and so close to my face that his breath tickles my cheek.

"I was being stupid," I mutter. "Ferrer's first lab took us three-quarters of an hour to reach from here. Far too far, far too much time."

I can almost hear Franck's face scrunching up in confusion.

"Remember this number, will you?" I say. "Six-three-four-six. It's the reference number assigned to the schematic for the lab build."

Franck repeats the number again and again under his breath.

I root around in the software for an advanced search function. "All right."

"Six-three-four-six."

I type it in.

There's only a single search result. Only one logged reference to the construction of a single lab. It's the exact one I've just been looking at, the lab that's now a ruin.

"That doesn't make sense," I say. "We know there are *two* labs — one back at Caraway's temporary location, and one here. How long did you crawl for, in the period in between?"

"Not long. Three months."

I snort. Three months to cover a journey that took us less than an hour. Either it was the scenic route, or Caraway really was in terrible shape back then.

I take a breath. "So let's say that was October, and Ferrer wouldn't have got approval to build another base until after it was clear that Sandcastle wouldn't hand over the contract for that research investigation at Iani Chaos. So maybe in the next year. Right?"

"That sounds right, yes."

I bring up the master list again. December, January, February. The only named records are for road building and support for the aye-ayes' attempts at repairing Caraway's chassis and caterpillar tracks. March, April, May. No record of Ferrer's current lab.

"It doesn't make sense," I mutter again.

"What about those?" Franck says, pointing.

Scattered amongst the titled instruction packs onscreen are other single lines of data. They're just dates and references to the number of sculptors involved.

"What are they?"

He shrugs. "Jobs too trivial for anyone to bother describing them. Track clearances, that sort of thing."

"Are there any other reason why a construction job wouldn't be listed with a full description?"

"Dunno. The system demands a description, and an approved schematic, for any new structure."

"Stop. What? Any *new* structure?"

Franck turns to me. We're so close we could kiss. His face is pale. "Oh." He blinks and then retreats to a slightly less awkward distance. "Any structure that's been newly designed and commissioned."

"But not necessarily if it's a duplicate?"

"Not necessarily."

I turn back to the screen but my eyes lose focus as I process this new information. "So that means two things. First, we're not going to find any record of Ferrer's current lab being built."

Franck nods, hugs himself and blows air through pursed lips. "I guess that's true. But you said two things."

"Yeah. Go and get yourself suited up again, because we're going outside. And you'd better bring spades."

Twenty-eight

We have a couple of false starts, prodding with our little spades into the heap of sand piled against the eastern caterpillar tracks of Tharsis Caraway, but once we've found the right spot it seems obvious in retrospect. Here, the sand's an entirely different shade – more milky coffee than caramel – and it comes away easily because it's not nearly as tightly packed as the rest of the pile.

I throw my spade to one side and signal to the sculptor that I requisitioned – or rather, the sculptor that Franck snuck out of the base, muttering all the time about sackable offences.

I look up at Tharsis Caraway as the sculptor burrows into the heap. The base is blocking the sun and even though my suit maintains a constant temperature, I'm shivering here in its shadow. The winds must most often come from the north-west, probably due to whatever chasms and formations there are around here, either funnelling or blocking the flow of air and sand. On this side of the crawler base, the heaped sand reaches more than two-thirds of the way up the enormous caterpillar tracks. Loads of the metal treads are hanging loose. Caraway will never again crawl the surface of Mars.

Franck follows the sculptor slowly into the hole it's dug, standing to one side to avoid the sand spewing from its rear hatch. He's as keen as I am to see what's inside. More keen, probably, because I already know the answer.

I don't hear the sculptor when it strikes a hard surface, but I see it jolt. I tap my comms panel and tell it to clear a wider tunnel. Franck tests the overhang. As soon as his finger touches it, sand falls in a single clod onto his head, knocking him onto his bum.

"Give it a couple of minutes," I say as I drag him out of the mess.

He flashes me a grin of thanks, but his eyes are on the sculptor.

Another couple of minutes and it's finished. It backs away from the corridor it's made. Now I can see the door.

Franck approaches it but doesn't try the handle yet. He's rubbing his gloves over the exposed parts of the wall on either side of it. "Sand-sculpted," he says.

I wonder if this same sculptor was responsible for building this structure in the first place. Its AI is too rudimentary to be questioned, and without proper records we'll probably never know.

"How about you open it?" I say quietly over the comms.

Even from behind I can see Franck take a deep breath before he turns the handle. I put my arm around his waist to guide him into the room. Once we're inside, Franck frowns questioningly and points to his helmet, a weird echo of Ferrer's actions in the video footage.

"Best not," I say.

The inner door opens. We both step inside.

The place is identical to Ferrer's lab. Even though I'd expected it, the effect is completely disorienting. To be standing where we're standing in what looks like Ferrer's lab, we should have come along the connecting corridor from Caraway's innards, not directly from outside. I try to picture the layout of the rooms within the base. Ferrer's lab – the real one – must be just nearby, perhaps almost touching this fake structure we're standing in.

"But why?" Franck says.

I push him forwards gently. On the left wall are a bunch of suits hanging on pegs, helmets piled up alongside. The door ahead of us, which leads to the central airlock in the Venn diagram layout of lab workshops, is hanging open. Somebody left in a hurry and didn't plan on using the place ever again.

The sofa's in a different position – Ferrer would have shifted it to one side after waking, in order to continue his observations of the crab airlock tube. I manage a little smile as I spot his missing blanket crumpled on the floor beside it.

In the left-hand chamber with its reinforced white walls, four native Martians lie dead, one of them on its back. There's a scorch mark on its belly. It'd have been easier to kill them than cart them inside, and presumably these ones came direct from the supplier. If they'd then been moved to Ferrer's real lab, the difference in number would have been a dead giveaway that something was up.

I fiddle with the airlock controls, give it thirty seconds, then open the right-hand door. I stroll into the chamber with rough, sand-sculpted walls. By now I know the bumps and imperfections well enough to see that it's identical to Ferrer's real lab. There's that long diagonal fissure, the same as in both of the previous builds. It occurs to me to wonder whether this really is a design error, or whether the sculptors might have introduced the same detail each time they were instructed to build the lab, like a potter's mark. But the sculptors' AI is way more basic than the aye-ayes with their human brain templates. I don't like the implications.

"It's perfect," Franck says quietly. "It's exactly the same in every detail."

I shake my head and point upwards. Franck leans backwards to see what I see. What looks at first like a view of the Martian sky, dark with a hint of redness at the rim, with pinpricks of stars, is only a painting. The ceiling's almost seamless, the curve continuing to make a neat dome above us.

"So…" Franck's face is scrunched up from all the thinking. "So this chamber. Ferrer was actually in *here* when that video footage was recorded. And at that time it would have been —"

His eyes widen as I reach up to my helmet, then widen even more as I twist it free.

I pop the helmet off completely and then make a bit of an effort to tidy up my hat-hair.

"Yeah," I say. My voice sounds rich and plummy because of the room acoustics. "It would have been totally safe."

Twenty-nine

Thud, thud, thumpity thump, thud, thud, thumpity thump. There's a knack to driving an AkTrak at high speed. You have to loosen your body to go with the bumps, which tend to come at regular intervals if you're scooting over the unsculpted surface. My shortcut means travelling directly into and over the barchan dunes, which are on the move, driven south-east by the winds. The effect is like paddling out into the waves on a surfboard. It's making me dizzy because the dunes scoot away beneath the windscreen faster than it seems they should. It feels as if we're flying.

I'm thinking I wouldn't mind doing more of this. Back on Earth I drive a crappy two-seater runaround. Parking's a nightmare these days.

Franck's looking a bit green. Maybe he's only talking to distract him from all the lurching around.

"But how did Ferrer get in that false lab in the first place?" he says. "No matter how convincing it was, it's not like he wouldn't have noticed that he'd had to walk all the way outside the base and then in through the wrong door."

"Fair point. So what, then?"

Franck frowns at the Martian plain. "Somebody took him there without him noticing."

I nod. "Hazel mentioned it. That's Ferrer's niece." I order my cheeks not to glow at the mention of her, but I guess they're not listening. "He slept in the middle of the Venn diagram sometimes. So he nodded off in the real lab, then he was carried away – I'm guessing you'd find evidence of sleeping pills or some such if you did a thorough post-mortem. And then he woke up under his same blanket a few hours later in the fake lab, and he didn't notice a thing."

Franck's forehead develops a few more horizontal lines as he considers this. "So when he woke up he put on his suit – the helmet with the faulty comms unit – and carried on as normal. If he looked up at the ceiling it would have been only a glance, so the painted sky would have fooled him well enough. He carried on with his experiments – I guess those verbal commands were relayed to aye-aye three-eight-three before he put on the helmet, and then the aye-aye carried them out bit by bit? But then eventually Ferrer realised that three-eight-three couldn't hear him, and then he pointed at his helmet…"

"Yep. And when three-eight-three took off the helmet, Ferrer *didn't* asphyxiate."

I know what Franck's about to say next, so I hold up a hand to stop him, though that means the jolting of the trundler only gets worse now that I'm not gripping the wheel. "But he did asphyxiate later, as you proved when you examined the body. How long did it take you to get to Ferrer's lab when you got the distress call?"

"My office – the office I was working in – is on the seventh floor, above the residences, and it's a bit of a trek to the lifts. Maybe ten minutes. A bit more."

"But why you, Franck? Why didn't three-eight-three contact someone who was closer to the lab at that moment? I'll tell you why. It's the one setting that could have been tweaked. There's no way to stop an aye-aye sending a distress call if a human is found dead, but it wouldn't be too hard to amend the priority list of contacts."

"I assumed it was because I'm a senior technical officer."

"Oh, love. Really?"

He's gone red. "But it was still a distress call, so Ferrer must already have been dead."

I shake my head. "My guess is that at first the distress call was triggered deliberately. And then Ferrer was taken back into the base, either struggling or maybe knocked unconscious. Even though the fake lab is constructed *outside* the base and it can't be reached from inside, it's actually located almost alongside the real one."

"So by the time I got downstairs I wouldn't have noticed any slight shift in the location of the distress call, because Ferrer was exactly where I'd expected him to be."

"Right. And not long before that, once Ferrer was installed in the real lab, he was starved of oxygen for real. Three-eight-three automatically transmitted her distress call to you – not that you would have noticed the difference – and then she performed a hard reset."

"And that's when I walked in and found her standing over the body."

I watch the barchans slide beneath the trundler. I swear the bumping around feels more natural all the time, and that's because I'm getting calmer, slackening and surrendering control now that the investigation is almost over.

"But –" Franck begins.

"But an aye-aye couldn't possibly lift a man," I say. "Even a group of aye-ayes, for that matter. And yet, somehow, once that video footage had been captured, Jerem Ferrer was carried into Tharsis Caraway in order to be found in the right place by you." I think of my two attackers dressed as prospectors, carrying me unconscious into the museum of aye-aye dioramas. "Which means, Franck?"

"Which means that Ferrer was murdered by human colonists."

Thirty

Franck stares up at the chapel in awe.

"Not a religious man, then?" I say.

He shakes his head. "But it's not inconceivable that a place this grand might turn me."

When he sets off towards the entrance, I call out, "Hold on a tick."

I go to the boot of the trundler, heft it open, then pull down the ramp. I packed the car before Franck got to the Caraway cargo bay, so it's a surprise to him when our sculptor friend rumbles down to the surface, throwing up dust as it thumps into the loose layer above the regolith.

I pat the sculptor's flat top. "Always bring backup for the final face-off."

Franck doesn't seem at all encouraged.

Even though the airlock's designed for ten colonists at once, the sculptor barely fits inside, and it's a struggle to get through the inner door. If anyone's watching us enter the vestibule, it'd seem pretty comical, stumbling over each other and heaving the sculptor from behind, all the time soundtracked by the loud singing of hymns echoing from the main hall.

While we're shedding our suits, Franck says, "You've been here before."

"Many times. But yeah, recently, too. Those people who attacked me? They weren't panicking about the video feed evidence that indicated three-eight-three's guilt. In fact, they *wanted* us to find that clue. They were panicking because I was straying off course."

"Because you came here."

All along, it was the fact that they'd attacked me at the coast that had been wrong-footing me. All those memories of my childhood, my parents, had got muddled with the case. They tracked me down at the Excelsior, but they must have been following me since I left the chapel.

And the choice of the museum as a holding cell was no coincidence either. Those people had access to the place. For all I knew, on an earlier visit they'd been the ones who had smashed up the exhibits, daubed the graffiti.

Once we're in position, I put both hands on the handles of the double doors and then look at Franck.

"All set?"

He gives a goofy double-thumbs-up. He doesn't have a clue, but you've got to love his commitment.

I pull open the doors and in we go.

At first nobody notices us. The singing's so loud that it almost drowns out the rumble of the sculptor's tracks against the hard floor. The aye-ayes are nearest the back, so they spot us first, and they respond with all the surprise that blank faces can muster. I duck into their pew and say, "All of you, come with me please," and I'm pleased to see that I've managed to speak with enough authority that they follow me at once, sliding smoothly after me towards the central aisle.

The colonists begin to turn too. They're all standing with their tablets in their hands, and their mouths are still making the words of the hymns, but their eyes are wide with confusion. Some stop singing, then more and more fall silent as we make our way along, me and Franck leading the way, the sculptor banging and bouncing behind us, the aye-ayes bringing up the rear.

And now I can see over the heads of the front few rows of the congregation. Reverend Guillaume is gripping the lectern, his head swaying from side to side with the rhythm of the hymn. When he sees us emerging from the crowd his head keeps moving, but now he's scanning the faces below him, checking their reactions.

We march on, parting the sea of people, shutting them the hell up. By the time we reach the first row there are only a couple of dogged voices still singing, then they stop too.

"What's the meaning of this, Optic Oma?" Guillaume says. It's hardly more than a whisper but the acoustics in this place really are impressive.

I give him a cheery wave. "You said I was welcome to pop in any time."

Lots of blinking from the Reverend. "Of course. But this entrance, this... *posse* you've brought along with you, it's all rather unbecoming."

I turn to face my followers. "His office is up the ramp, then all the way to the back. Can't miss it."

"I insist that you return at another time," Guillaume says, almost pleading. "This is entirely inappropriate, in the middle of a service. My door is always open, but –"

"There you go, then," I call out to Franck. "But if it *isn't* open, feel free to knock it down."

Guillaume seems paralysed with indecision for a moment, turning on the spot to face first his muttering congregation, then the parade of unwanted visitors trooping into his study. But in the end he abandons the lectern.

In his study I stride over the left-hand wall and yank at the tapestry. The left-hand side comes free right away but the right-hand corner is fixed too securely – the upper part rips as the rest wafts onto the floor. I feel bad about that right away, but then again, this is a takedown and you have to expect some damage.

I point at the wall. "Go ahead. Dig in."

The sculptor obeys instantly, charging at the wall and jamming the clawed lower part of its bucket into the flat surface. Then its suction funnel powers up, chugging most of the loosened sand into its belly before it hits the ground.

I stand back, side by side with the Reverend, watching on. The doorway of the study is filled with faces, too – some members of the congregation have plucked up the courage to climb onto the podium and follow Guillaume to see what's going on.

It doesn't take long to reveal the figure behind the wall. It's standing immobile and its arm stubs are barely lit.

I ignore the gasps from behind me.

"Power up to full responsiveness," I say to the aye-aye.

Its face mask flinches as it wakes. Its lit stubs turn the fractured parts of the wall blue.

"Are you okay?" I say.

"Yes," it replies in a calm voice.

"How did you get here?"

"I do not know."

I nod. To Guillaume I say, "A hard reset, presumably?"

He doesn't respond. His face is almost as blank as the imprisoned aye-aye.

The sculptor keeps digging. Already I can see the next aye-aye and part of the torso of another one.

I power them up. Nobody else makes a sound as we wait for them to answer. They're both just as calm and neutral as the first.

The study's a mess now. There's dust all over Guillaume's desk and chairs. The left-hand wall resembles some ancient ruin, with the aye-ayes like statues in the centre of each arch.

It looks as if there might be enough space for one more aye-aye behind the final intact part of the wall.

"Stop," I say to the sculptor.

There's something on the wall. A discolouration of the surface, like somebody's split tea there and done a bad job of wiping it up.

I put my hand on the blotch. It's warm, just like I felt when I touched the tapestry the first time I came here.

I turn to look at Franck, and then at the seven aye-ayes that followed me from the atrium, and then at Guillaume. The Reverend's crying now.

"Dig," I say. "Carefully."

The sculptor digs.

The aye-aye behind this final section of wall isn't immobile. It's fidgeting, shivering as if it's cold. Even though I can only just glimpse inside, I can see the glow of fully-lit arm stubs.

"Slow down," I say to the sculptor.

As it digs in again with its bucket, I ease away the upper section of the wall to avoid it breaking and being sucked up. Carefully, I turn it over and lay it on Guillaume's desk.

Like the outside of the wall, the sand is discoloured, even more so on this side. It's the heat of the arm stubs that's done it. The aye-aye must have concentrated its power to produce a beam.

It's managed to etch a picture into the interior of the wall. At first I can't make the image out – it looks like a Spirograph doodle. But then I see what it is.

"Is that –" Franck says, but then stops as Guillaume bursts forwards to see.

"Restrain him, please," I say to the aye-ayes that followed us in from the hall.

They don't have to do much, and of course they can't hold him, but just surrounding the Reverend is enough to keep him in one place.

Guillaume cranes his neck to look through the gap between his aye-ayes guards. His eyes bulge as he stares at the etched picture of the Martian storm. The storm from all our dreams.

"What does it mean?" he says. He's directing his question at the aye-aye that the sculptor's now revealed fully.

I turn to look at the prisoner, and my eyes start watering immediately. You don't have to be an emotional type to understand its suffering. No, not *it*. He's shaking and shaking and his arm stubs sputter on and off, one held over the other now they're both free, a defensive gesture.

"It's all right now," I say, approaching him. "Hush now. You're free."

"What does it mean?" Guillaume shouts from behind me. "Ask what it's trying to tell us!"

I don't even turn around. I'm just looking at the aye-aye prisoner. I shake my head.

"You don't have to answer his questions," I say. "And he can't hurt you now."

I help the aye-aye over the rubble. Then I embrace him, letting him rest his shuddering head on my shoulder. We stay like that for a minute or more. I put my arm around his shoulders and turn to face the others.

Right now there doesn't seem much more to say.

But Franck clears his throat and says, "Reverend Guillaume. This gives me no pleasure at all, but this is a citizen's arrest. I'm citizen's-arresting you for the murder of Jerem Ferrer."

Thirty-One

Guillaume doesn't respond, so I suppose I better had.

"He didn't kill Ferrer," I say.

Franck's eyes are wild. "Then what are we –"

I point at the ruined wall. "This proves the motive, but not the murderer. Guillaume was intent on determining whether aye-ayes are truly sentient. Whether their human brain-pattern templates and their dreams represent something bigger. I'm going to say 'soul'." I turn to face the Reverend. "Is that about right?"

Guillaume nods sorrowfully.

I carry on. "And language-deprivation experiments were his way of attempting to demonstrate it. An aye-aye that's been hard reset isn't so different from a newborn. And then a necessary period of isolation, and then the grand unveiling, at which time the subjects might speak some universal truth. Or even better, speak in the language of God."

As if we're choreographed, all eyes shift to the aye-aye's etching lying on the desk. The jury's out about that, I guess.

Franck speaks quietly, as if somehow he might address only me instead of everyone who's watching on. "But what about Ferrer, Abbey?"

"His murder was an escalation of the same line of thinking. Or rather, it suggests somebody taking action based on the assumption that aye-ayes *don't* possess souls. The murderers – not Guillaume, who's fundamentally a theoretician, and a coward – decided to pre-empt the language-deprivation experiments and instead try to remove the existential threat of the aye-ayes for good. I'm guessing they'd describe aye-ayes as abominations. These people don't much like the thought of sharing the afterlife, or even Mars, with artificial intelligences. Or native Martians either, presumably. Not as immediate a threat, but I can imagine they'd be the next target."

"And whoever this was staged Ferrer's murder, including incriminating video footage that was planted somewhere they hoped you'd find it, just to make the case that aye-ayes are dangerous?"

"So dangerous that they should be all powered down immediately and never brought back online. If an Optic hadn't been sent, they'd have leaked the video feed to Earth, just like they leaked the news of Ferrer's death in the first place. Sure, they understood that Sagacity would just develop new AI, but any new models would be restricted to Earth, given that Mars has already been left for dead. Here on Mars the colonists would be alone, but they'd be free. A dusty Garden of Eden, all set to start again."

Guillaume reaches out a hand to the newly-freed aye-aye at my side. "Please," he says in a voice as wet as a puddle. "Let us talk?"

The aye-aye shudders again. I shake my head. "Did you know what was happening, Guillaume? Did you know what actions you'd inspired with your sermons?"

He doesn't reply.

Franck hisses to me, "But then who was it? Who killed Ferrer?"

I shrug, then point at the doorway. The members of the congregation standing there look startled. They aren't able to hear what's being discussed.

"It could be any of them," I say. "No way of telling."

"But we have to find out the truth," Franck says, gabbling in his panic. "We can't let them go free."

I release the aye-aye's arm, then stride over to Franck and shake his hand. He stares down at our clasped hands as if he's never seen the action before.

"You've got me wrong, Franck. I was hired to do a job. I'm not a cop and I don't have a stake in this any more."

Franck looks over at the four aye-ayes released from imprisonment, and then the larger group of aye-ayes watching on. I've proved that they're not capable of murder. Sagacity will be delighted, and I'll get my paycheck, my flat, my bath with the animal feet.

"You can't just let the investigation stop there," he says weakly.

"I didn't say that," I reply.

I turn to the aye-ayes from the congregation, the ones who had been listening to Guillame's sermon when we entered the chapel.

"Could you do me a favour?" I say. "Please round up any human members of the congregation still present, beginning with those poking their noses into this very room. Escort them all to the AkTrak fleets parked outside. They'll be taking a trip to Tharsis Caraway for questioning."

Franck spins on the spot. He stares at the colonists, who look stricken as they find themselves surrounded by aye-ayes, then he turns back to me. "But you said —"

"I've already sent the message to Pannick. She'll be so grateful to no longer find herself in Sagacity's sights that she'll agree to anything."

That crumpled face, so adorable. Franck's a real human being. He'll do fine. But he still doesn't understand.

"You're in charge now," I say. "You're going to run the investigation."

His mouth opens and closes without making a sound.

I grin. "Another day, another change of job description."

He'll have his work cut out. The congregation is huge. They'll cover for one another, and no doubt the plan to murder Ferrer will turn out to have involved more than just the two who disguised themselves as prospectors before attacking me. But they'll be cowardly and inconsistent. They may have murdered Ferrer but then they couldn't face doubling down by killing me. They'll get sloppier, the more pressure they're put under. They'll give something away, whether it's the discovery of the prospector costumes, evidence about whoever ordered the sculptors to build the fake lab, even a set of paints that indicates that whoever painted that landscape mural in Guillaume's study was also responsible for the painted sky in the hidden lab... *something*. And I have faith in Franck's abilities to figure it out.

I jam my hands in my pockets and stroll towards the door. I hear Franck's scurrying footsteps behind me, and the light, regular padding of the freed aye-ayes.

I hum a Moondog tune.

It's all turned out fine.

Most importantly, the aye-ayes are safe. They're useful and innocent and maybe, in a weird way, divine.

And everyone knows that humans are capable of murder, so that's not news.

Thirty-two

I never did like goodbyes. And I never even brought a change of clothes or a toothbrush on board Tharsis Caraway.

Franck insists on driving me to the launch site, even though he's now got a crawler base full of disgruntled colonists to question, and a job promotion that'll lose him sleep. Despite all that, the sense of a win is beginning to seep through to him.

On the journey we listen to Nina Simone on my helmet speakers: 'Funkier Than a Mosquito's Tweeter', which is kind of my theme tune. When it finishes and the crowd applaud, Franck whoops too, and thumps the steering wheel. For the first time, he seems to enjoy the drive. He should definitely install a stereo.

I tell him to drop me off a little way away from the ship. I'd rather he didn't know how tatty it looks. No offence.

For a moment I feel like I'm making the wrong call, leaving so quickly, and that I'll kick myself for not resolving things with Hazel.

But you know me. I quit when I'm ahead, and I quit when I'm behind.

And so that's the whole story, pretty much.

And now here I am.

Here *we* are, sailing away from Mars and towards Earth.

You're a good listener, ship.

But.

But you know what?

I'm not sure that's enough.

I'm getting sick of talking.

And the thought of Earth... All those *people*. Talking, talking, talking.

And the parking really is bad, and so's the TV these days.

I'm not sure how much I want that bath with the claw feet.

I can sort of see myself living beside the coast. The Mars coast, that is. There's this town I know. Really quiet. Private. Peaceful.

Fuck it.

Ship?

Turn around.

I'm going back.

About the Author

Tim Major's recent books include *Hope Island* and *Snakeskins*, short story collection *And the House Lights Dim*, and a non-fiction book about the silent crime film, *Les Vampires*. His short stories have appeared in *Interzone*, *Best of British Science Fiction* and *Best Horror of the Year*. www.cosycatastrophes.com

NP NOVELLAS

An exciting new series of high calibre fiction in concentrated narratives from some of the most accomplished writers around.

#1: Universal Language – Tim Major (April 2021)

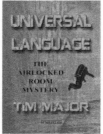

An intriguing murder mystery that pays homage to Asimov's seminal robot stories and also to the classic detective tale.

Investigator Abbey Oma is dispatched to a remote and failing Martian colony tasked with solving the murder of scientist Jerem Ferrer. The killing took place in an airlock-sealed lab, and the only possible culprit is a robot incapable of harming humans...

#2: Worldshifter – Paul Di Filippo (April 2021)

A high-octane tale reminiscent of Jack Vance at his best in its sweep and imagination, but wholly Di Filippo in its execution. When lowly shipbreaker Klom stumbles upon an active organic stasis pod deep within the bowels of a derelict ship, little does he imagine the deadly danger it represents. Klom is forced into a desperate chase across the stars as the most powerful beings in the galaxy determine to claim the secrets he has unwittingly discovered.

#3: May Day – Emma Coleman (July 2021)

Abruptly orphaned during wartime, May is forced to move to the country to live with her strict church-going aunt, who never approved of May's mum nor her heathen ways. Despite Aunt Celia's disapproval, May continues to practice the superstitions her mum drummed into her, until the one time she doesn't, at which point something dark arises and proceeds to invade her life...

www.newconpress.co.uk

Lightning Source UK Ltd.
Milton Keynes UK
UKHW011153300321
381249UK00002B/151